Subversive Stories

The Parables as Modern Short Stories

David Elston

ISBN-13: 979-8-9894776-3-0

Shreveport Biblical Counseling
670 Albemarle Dr, Suite 1200
Shreveport, LA 71106

Cover art licensed from Adobe Stock
Cover design by David Elston

Shreveport
Biblical
Counseling

CYPRESS PRESS

an independent publisher

Dedicated to

Jess
who has spent the last fifteen years
trying to convince me I have a
Talent
and giving me the courage
not to bury it

Parables & Stories

Introduction

SOMETIMES I GET BORED OF THE TRUTH. There, I said it. Overfamiliar with its voice, I yawn and fall asleep. I build up a resistance and become dead to its touch. This was also true of the people to whom Jesus preached and was the reason, I believe, he told the parables.

Parables come at us sideways. The truth is still present, but it's shy, having hidden itself in a story, no longer preaching but merely hinting and gesturing, only showing its face when it must. In a parable the truth disguises itself in characters who pull at our sleeves, begging to be heard and understood. It sneaks around in a plot like a child with a guilty smile, and you can't help but ask, "What are you up to, you little devil?" Camouflaged in drama, parables make us feel, lowering our defenses and making us vulnerable. Thus, while our imagination is busy and distracted and caught up with the story, without knowing it, the truth slips in the back door and makes itself at home in our hearts. Hence the name of this book, "Subversive Stories."

Literally translated from Greek, a parable is "cast

alongside." Parables are not like other truth-telling methods. Preaching aims to proclaim. Teaching aims to clarify and organize. Parables, however, are indirect. Rather than hitting you between the eyes like a good sermon, a parable fights dirty, attacking you from behind when you aren't looking. It is willing to forego some of its clarity for the sake of creativity. It gives up the right to proclaim and goes undercover as a story about everyday things. But make no mistake, in the hands of Jesus, such "subversive" tactics are used with the most loving and trustworthy intentions. The point of this book is to follow after him in this, interpreting and expanding his parables into modern short stories. May these stories, like his parables, help those like me who are prone to becoming dull and dead towards the truth. And when we turn around and find the truth having crept back into our hearts, may we greet it with pleasant surprise, as a long-lost friend rather than an intruder.

Allow me a few notes to help you read these parabolic stories well and get the most out of them.

First, like the parables, these are symbolic stories, but they are not allegories. You will waste your time and probably ruin the experience if you try to interpret every single bit of the story as something laden with spiritual truth. Yes, there are many symbolic characters, and there are conversations that are full of biblical meaning. At the same time, most of the stories are driving home one particular point - hopefully the same point as the parable it is based on. The peripherals are just part of the story. Sometimes, as Hemingway once said, the fish is just a fish. The best way to avoid making this mistake is simply to read the parables before reading the story. That should provide you with "antennae" for what's important as you read. I've tried to stick as close as I can to the original people, plots, and points of Jesus' parables.

Second, similar to the parables, the contents of these stories are drawn from everyday, ordinary life. For Jesus, this included things like farming, fishing, family, and even "church." In doing so he puts the truth into terms that are familiar and domestic, understandable by anyone with ears to hear. The stories in this book are, likewise, drawn from everyday 21st century life (admittedly with a Louisiana flavor).

Despite their ordinary content, Jesus could be provocative in his parables, borrowing from the more sordid parts of first century life things like violence, robbery, racism, and prostitution. Some of his comparisons are likewise provocative. Jesus gives a lesson on persistent prayer with a parable about an old lady who won't quit nagging an unjust judge. He likens the kingdom of Almighty God to a tiny mustard seed. He tells us to imitate a dishonest manager who swindles his boss. Such provocative methods are part of the subversion. They are meant to "provoke" - to rub you the wrong way and wake you up, to get your blood pumping. These stories you are about to read are, likewise, provocative. They are not without their share of drugs, sex, drunkenness, and murder. I've been careful not to be graphic or glorifying, but they are meant to be provocative. I have tried my best not to include any two-dimensional flannelgraph Sunday school characters.

As stories tend to do, you may experience a range of emotions reading this book. Some stories might make you laugh. Some frustrate you. Most readers will be offended at some point, though for the best possible reasons. Some of these may stir compassion in you for the most unlikely people. There is one story in particular that I have not been able to get through without tears, either in writing or editing it. Isn't it amazing that we can get so worked up over people and events that aren't even real? Whatever the emotion, to feel is to be vulnerable, which is another reason Jesus spoke truth in parables. When we are emotional, we are susceptible to persuasion.

In sum, by reading these stories, you are signing up for subversion. But be encouraged: if I have done it well, it will not be *my* truth, but Truth himself who sneaks his way into your heart.

Well, I hope I have not oversold it. I'll let you get to it. He who has ears to hear, let him hear...

PART I
PARABLES OF GRACE

THE PARABLE OF THE PHARISEE & TAX COLLECTOR
Luke 18:9-14

"He also told this parable to some who trusted in themselves that they were righteous, and treated others with contempt: 'Two men went up into the temple to pray, one a Pharisee and the other a tax collector. The Pharisee, standing by himself, prayed thus: 'God, I thank you that I am not like other men, extortioners, unjust, adulterers, or even like this tax collector. I fast twice a week; I give tithes of all that I get.' But the tax collector, standing far off, would not even lift up his eyes to heaven, but beat his breast, saying, 'God, be merciful to me, a sinner!' I tell you, this man went down to his house justified, rather than the other. For everyone who exalts himself will be humbled, but the one who humbles himself will be exalted.'"

Too Far Gone

GEORGE PETERSON WOKE UP PROMPTLY AT 5:30 AM. He put on his robe and slippers and went into the kitchen, where he poured himself a cup of coffee with a teaspoon of cream, no sugar. As he did so, he was pleased with himself for remembering to program the coffee the night before. He sat down in his armchair in the living room, opened his Bible to where he left off the day before, and began to read Proverbs 12. He had a little notebook where he would jot a verse and a prayer related to his reading.

Today he wrote, "'A good man obtains favor from the Lord,' and prayed, "Thank you for your favor, O Lord."

At 6:00, George set his Bible aside, marking his place. He left his notebook of prayers open on the side table where his wife would see them. He stood upright. Still a little tight from the triathlon he was training for, he bent over and stretched his hamstrings, reaching all the way to his toes - something, he thought to himself, not many grown men can do.

He opened the curtains of the living room windows. The first light of the morning was dawning onto his yard. He noted his weedless, mulched flower beds, the carefully shaped boxwoods, and the smoothly mown grass. Although he did not cut his own grass nor tend the beds, he was satisfied with having a yard that was so well-maintained. He poured another cup of coffee and stepped out the front door onto the porch to admire his yard a little further. When he did so, he couldn't help but notice the clear line of demarcation between his yard and his neighbors. He looked with a mixture of pity and annoyance at the yard on his right. *Well, at least they tried,* George thought to himself with a little smile, *but clearly they haven't a clue about proper lawn care.* The grass was brown in some spots, the edging was unevenly done with a weed eater, and there was crabgrass and bull thistle scattered throughout the lawn. *I suppose that's what happens when you have five children.*

Next, George looked at the yard to the left. *Good Lord!* The grass was knee-high. Unkempt bushes and unidentifiable weeds covered most of the windows. Limbs that had fallen in the dry spell last month were laying across the yard. One had even knocked off some of the fascia board from the house, which had yet to be replaced. *Perhaps I should get Pedro to do her yard too. Just this once. Why not? I certainly have the means. I'm known to be a charitable man. I think that's just what I'll do.* George felt good about the decision. *Besides,* he thought, *it's bringing down property values.*

As George waxed in self-esteem on his porch, Trixie, whose yard he was observing, drove up the street and pulled into her driveway. He took a slow sip of coffee and watched while she lingered in her car. *Another one-night stand, I'd bet.* After a while she opened the car door and stumbled out, dropping a few things as she did so. *Dear God, I think she's inebriated.* Trixie did not stop and pick them up but walked to her front door with her head down, muttering to herself and shaking as she tried to unlock her door. He waited for her to look at him so that he could give her a nod and smile, perhaps even say good morning, but she did not notice him. He felt slighted and reconsidered his former decision. *No, if I help I will only be enabling her lifestyle. She's got to suffer the consequences. Oh well, she's probably too far gone anyway.* More clearly than ever, he saw how different he was from Trixie. *Thank you, O Lord.* His moment of gratitude was interrupted by the sight of a weed in his flowerbed. Unnerved but composed, he headed inside to call Pedro about the weed and then prepare for his Sunday school lesson.

The night before, Trixie came home alone. It was almost midnight, and she had just finished a double shift, waitressing during the day, bartending at night. It was her fourth double that week, and she was exhausted, but it was the only way to make a dent in her credit card debt. Yet, the money and the debt were not what was on her mind that night.

It was a Saturday night and, for most of her adult life, that had meant a party. It meant friends, relaxing at someone's house to watch a game or perhaps heading downtown to a club. It also meant a substance of some kind, ordinarily nothing more than jello shots or a few hits of a bong, but after a really rough week of work, when the need to party was great, it would not take much convincing for her to up the ante. Her drug of choice depended on the kind of week she'd had. Some weeks she might crush up a Xanax, snort it, and melt into the comfort of a friend's couch. Other weeks she and a friend might dissolve a tab of LSD on their tongues and fly off into a wonderland. But that was not what was on her mind that Saturday night either.

In all those previous years of Saturday nights, the hope was always to head home with a man. And often, she did. When she was young it was always someone different. The next morning, hungover or perhaps still drunk, she would wake early and stagger out of the house, careful not to wake him. The few that managed to get her number would reach out to her in the days following, but she never responded. She was not interested in commitment, she told herself. When she got into her thirties, however, and the number of available bachelors dwindled, she began seeing the same handful of guys. Now, at forty-two, the only one still interested in her was a man named Chad.

That Saturday, having worked so many hours, Trixie felt like she deserved a little something and picked up some chicken wings on the way home. Taking a beer from the refrigerator, she sat down at the kitchen bar and ate the lukewarm wings and fries from the styrofoam container. Not having received any calls or messages during her shifts, she scrolled casually through social media on her phone, seeing what she expected. Families at the beach. Couples celebrating anniversaries. Regina going on a rant. A group of girlfriends partying on a getaway cruise.

That Saturday night she was too exhausted to party. She had no drugs on hand, legal or otherwise, and wasn't in a financial place to run up a tab at a bar. Besides, she was starting to feel out of place at the clubs, too old to belong. More than anything that Saturday night, she was lonely.

She texted Chad.

"You awake?"

. . .

"Yep. Ready when you are."

His brazen assumption made her angry. She didn't respond for a bit and thought of calling it off. When she finished her beer and wings, Trixie looked around her dimly lit home and tried to think of something better to do, anything. She looked at what movies were streaming and found nothing she hadn't seen already. She was too stressed to sleep. It was too late to call a friend. *Oh well, anything is better than going to see that loser.* Still in her work clothes, she laid on the couch and stared at the ceiling. In the quiet of her home her thoughts began to wander. Eventually she found herself thinking, not of Chad, but of the feeling she had with any man when, after it was all said and done, for just a moment, he held her.

"On my way," she responded.

About five hours later, she left Chad's garage apartment without waking him, stumbling down the stairs. She got in her car but sat for a while without turning it on, staring ahead. She looked over at Chad's mustang and felt like keying the side of it, but then she thought to herself, *You're no different than him. What right do you have?* She hit the dashboard with her fist instead and said, "What is *wrong* with me?" Finally turning the car on, she backed out of the driveway.

On her way home, Trixie rolled down the window and lit a cigarette. She flipped aimlessly through the local radio stations, looking for something to fill the silence. Finding nothing good, she turned it off and began talking to herself. "Seriously though, what *is* wrong with you?" She laughed and answered herself,

"You're a whore, that's what. It's that simple." She glanced at herself in the rearview mirror. "Oh God, I really do look like a prostitute. Look at me! The raccoon eyes, the rouge, the ratty hair."

Just before she turned onto her street, she passed by St. Mary Magdalene's, a tiny Anglican church that she had driven by a thousand times. Driving slowly past, she noted the stone walls, stained glass windows, and arched roof. She was moved for a moment by its beauty in the soft, early sunlight, but the feeling didn't last. She felt the grime and filth of the bar on her skin. *Get real, honey, that's a holy place.* She looked away and was about to continue driving when her eye caught a statue in front of the church. It was a bronze statue of a man, welcoming people inside. She had seen it before, but until now had never noticed the ragged woman at the man's feet. She took a long drag on her cigarette and studied the two figures. She felt it once again, that longing to be held. Near the doors of the church, a man in a suit noticed her idling on the road and began to walk toward her with a smile and a wave. Alarmed, she flicked the cigarette, shifted into drive and sped away.

A few minutes later she pulled into her driveway and saw in the morning light what she could not see the night before. A rundown house, a yard full of weeds, and, more clearly than ever, herself. She leaned on her steering wheel and, for the first time in many years, began to cry. She wept over her night, over the many Saturdays she'd tried to escape from her life, over all the Chads that had held her over the years. The tears seemed to cleanse her mind. For the first time, she saw it all for what it was and was willing to let it go. *But what if I'm too far gone?* she thought.

Then she remembered the statue. Her skin tingled, and she wept again, but no longer in grief. Grabbing her purse, she got out of her car, unaware of the makeup bag that spilled onto the driveway. She unlocked the front door and headed inside, shaking with exhaustion and hope.

Questions

1. How does George resemble the Pharisee in the parable? Do you resemble George in any way?

2. Trixie is a mess. Describe her sin and suffering. What did you feel as you read about her? Are there any ways you are similar to Trixie?

3. What were the statues Trixie saw in front of the church? Why did they mean something to her?

4. In the parable, the tax collector, rather than the Pharisee, goes home justified. What evidence do you see that Trixie might be right with God by the end of the story? How is this different from the evidence of salvation you might normally look for?

5. Who was Jesus' telling the parable to (v. 9)? Why is this important?

Subversive Stories

The Parable of the Wedding Banquet
Luke 14:15-24

"When one of those who reclined at table with [Jesus] heard these things, he said to him, "Blessed is everyone who will eat bread in the kingdom of God!" But he said to him, "A man once gave a great banquet and invited many. And at the time for the banquet he sent his servant to say to those who had been invited, 'Come, for everything is now ready.' But they all alike began to make excuses. The first said to him, 'I have bought a field, and I must go out and see it. Please have me excused.' And another said, 'I have bought five yoke of oxen, and I go to examine them. Please have me excused.' And another said, 'I have married a wife, and therefore I cannot come.' So the servant came and reported these things to his master. Then the master of the house became angry and said to his servant, 'Go out quickly to the streets and lanes of the city, and bring in the poor and crippled and blind and lame.' And the servant said, 'Sir, what you commanded has been done, and still there is room.' And the master said to the servant, 'Go out to the highways and hedges and compel people to come in, that my house may be filled. For I tell you, none of those men who were invited shall taste my banquet.'"

An Unexpected Party

ANGELICA, AN ONLY CHILD, WAS TURNING TWELVE. Her long-awaited party was approaching. This was the first party she'd had since she was eight, a fact she often recited to her mother and father. By doing so, she was able to generate so much guilt in her parents that they promised not only a party, but one of such magnificence that it would not be forgotten for many years. As you will see, her parents were undeniably successful, but in a way that no one expected.

The day the invitations were sent out, Angelica came home from school and asked her mother if anyone had responded. "Not yet, sweetie," her mother said.

"You're joking," Angelica replied.

"They just went out today. I know it's hard to wait," her mother said, "but the party is still three weeks away." Angelica let out a guttural moan and stormed out of the room.

This pattern continued day after day. "Any replies to the invitation?" she'd ask. "Not yet, dear," her mother would say. With each passing day Angelica's moans deepened, and the storms intensified. At the two-week mark, there were still no RSVPs. Just before slamming her bedroom door, she shouted, "Aren't you going to DO something? Don't you care?" Each night, as her father put her into bed with her stuffies, she would close her eyes, put her hands together and say, "Dear God, I can't expect everyone to care about my party, but I know you do. Please, don't let me down."

In this way, Angelica manipulated her parents, berating her mother by day and burdening her father's conscience by night. She thought her parents were heartless and inconsiderate of her feelings.

In truth, her mother and father were filled with fear and desperation. There was a reason they hadn't thrown parties in recent years: at her eighth birthday party, no one had shown up. Angelica was so embarrassed, and they were so heartbroken, that her parents swore to one another never to let it happen again. The last three years they avoided the dilemma altogether by taking her on trips instead. Yet, they had only delayed the inevitable. Now, as they neared her upcoming party, their fears seemed to be proving true.

Her mother began calling her classmates' parents one by one.

"You should come, we'll have food trucks!" she said.

"Sorry," Georgia's mom said, "We're gluten-free."

"You should come, we'll have a bounce house!" her mother said.

"Sorry, Heidi says those are for babies."

"You should come, we're doing a raffle for an Xbox!" her mother said.

"Sorry," Violet's father said, "She's grounded."

"You should come, we'll have an ice cream bar!"

"Sorry," Michael's mom said, "He's lactose intolerant."

"You should come, we'll have a dunking booth!" her mother said.

"Sorry," Tommy's mom said, "He just doesn't want to."

Of course, none of these were the real reasons for their absence (except for Tommy). The truth of the matter was simply this: Angelica was weird. She did not know it, for she thought everyone else was the problem. But there was no denying it, Angelica was a universal misfit, though no one could agree on their reason for disliking her.

"Mom, she's like, *such* a spoiled brat," Georgia said.

"Dad, she's a big fat cusser," Heidi said.

"No way," said Violet, "She's got a reputation."

"Ugh," said Michael, "Mouth breather."

"She tried to kiss me last week at lunch," said Tommy. "I'm literally going to kill her if you make me go."

With a week left, Angelica's father decided to widen the scope, inviting not just her so-called friends but the entire seventh grade. Angelica was pleased to find this out, but in the end it only increased her rage when none of the one hundred fifty five seventh graders responded.

"I'm sure people will come," her mother told her. "You're such a gem. How could they not?"

"People are bad about RSVPs," her father said. "Don't worry, princess, they'll be here."

The night before the party, her parents laid awake, staring at the ceiling in the dark. Her mother held her husband's hand and wept. "What are we going to do?"

After a long time, her father finally said, "I've got a plan. Leave it to me."

It was Saturday, the long-awaited day of the party. The event was not until three o' clock. Waking before dawn, her father made signs and placed them around the neighborhood. "Block party! Bring a friend!" one sign said. "Free Philly Cheesesteaks," another sign said. "Yard games! Cake walks! Every child gets a prize!" He made many such signs, advertising to every kind of person he could imagine.

At eleven, the bounce house crew came, set up, and left.

At twelve thirty, a truck dropped off the dunking booth and filled it with water.

At one thirty, Angelica's mother picked up the ice cream cake. She made the goodie bags and put the drinks in the ice chests.

At two, the food trucks arrived and began to prep for the party.

Finally, three o' clock. Angelica stood outside on the driveway, waiting. "Mom!" she called at 3:02. "Where *are* they?"

"They'll be here!" she said nervously.

"Dad!" she called at 3:08. "You said they'd be here!"

"Don't worry, honey," he said. "I'm working on it."

Finally, at 3:15, the first guests arrived, a woman with seven children.

"Who are *you?*" Angelica said. "You're not in my class."

"We saw the sign about the slip and slide," they said, running past her. Angelica shrugged, somewhat pleased.

At 3:15, more guests arrived, a Chinese woman and her

daughter. And right behind them, a black woman.

"Who are *you?*" Angelica said. "I don't know you."

"We just move here," the Chinese woman said. "I bring *jiaozi.*"

Barely audible, the little girl beside her said, "*Jiaozi* means dumplings." She averted her eyes when Angelica looked at her.

"Girl, you look like a dumplin' yo'self," the black woman said. "I might just eat you up."

Angelica nodded and let them pass.

At 3:20, an old man arrived.

"Who are *you?*" Angelica said to him.

The old man let out an exasperated sigh. "Lordy mercy, impudent child," he said without looking at her. He walked past her toward the party. "And look at all this *extravagance.* Downright shameful. Never *heard* of such."

"Hmph," Angelica said with a slight smile.

When she was turned around, watching the children on the slip and slide, a lady walked up behind her with thick glasses and a perm. "Tell me, do you have any cats? Mine are so lonely and are due for some socialization."

"Yeah, yeah, go ahead," Angelica said. Confused, but encouraged by the guests so far, Angelica stayed at the end of the driveway awaiting more, but none came.

"Dad!" she called.

"Yes, dear?"

"We've got room for, like, fifty more."

"Don't worry, honey, I'm working on it," he said. He got into his car and turned onto the street. He drove onto the next block and began to knock at each house. Most of them didn't answer the door, but a few did.

"Hi, I live a street over. We're having a party. You know, food, games, free stuff. Would love for you to come."

Most of them weren't interested, but a few were.

"Are there chicken wings?" said a short young man with bloodshot eyes and a shaved head.

"No, but there's gourmet hot dogs."

He called over his shoulder to his friends. "Y'all want some grub?"

"Sure, Big D," they said, piling out of the house smelling like skunks.

At another house, a man with a US Marines flag in his window opened the door suspiciously. He was shirtless and had a hook for a left hand.

"What's the catch?" he said with a glare, pushing the screen door open a little with his hook.

"No catch, just fun and games. There's a dunking booth."

"Can I dunk you?"

"I guess."

"Be right there," he said, turning and going back inside. Across his back were tattooed the words, *Semper Fi.*

A few houses down, a middle-aged woman with heavy makeup and a low-cut blouse opened the door.

"Who all is there?" she asked.

"All sorts of people," he said.

"What about George? If he goes, I'll go. He lives across the street."

Angelica's father crossed the street and invited George to the party. George looked nervously across the street. "Got any beer?"

"No, sorry."

"I think I'll stay put," he said.

"Wait," Angelica's father said, putting a hand on the door as he was closing it. "I've got some in the fridge in the garage, take as many as you want."

"Thanks," George said, shutting the door behind him and walking down the street. The woman in the blouse and makeup followed soon after.

Angelica's father was concerned there weren't more people her age. He drove around for a bit until he came across a group of middle schoolers smoking cigarettes behind some bushes in the back of an empty parking lot. They flicked them away as he drove near. "Tell you what," he said, pulling to a stop. "Go to my daughter's birthday party and I won't tell your parents about the cigarettes." They looked at each other, shrugged and nodded. They got on their bikes and skateboards and rode down the street to the party.

Angelica continued greeting the guests. She did not understand who these people were or why they were coming to her party, but nevertheless her joy increased with each arrival. After the middle schoolers on the bikes arrived, smelling of cigarette smoke, she was content. The party was full, and she could now enjoy herself. As she turned and began walking toward all her new friends, she stopped, struck that not one of her guests was alike.

"Short and squat," she said, pointing at one, "Tall and wimpy," she said, pointing to another. She laughed in delight. It became a kind of game to her, pointing out all the varieties of people.

"Loud and rude," she said and then pointed toward another. "Quiet and mousy."

"Old and mean ... Young and shy," she said.

She pointed at her guests one by one, taking a moment to find the right word to describe them. "Loner ... loser ... floozy ... foul-mouthed ... show-off ... stinky ... fruitcake ... freaky . .. geezer ... pothead ... meathead," she laughed and clapped her hands.

Her dad, having just arrived home, walked up and began to listen to her. "Honey, you really shouldn't talk about people like that. Or point at them. It's rude."

"No, I don't mean it like that. It's just that ...They're," she said, turning and looking her father in the eyes. "They're like me." For the first time in her life, Angelica knew what it was to belong. For the first time in her life, Angelica accepted that she was weird, a universal misfit.

"Does that mean ... Are you happy with your party?" her father asked her.

"Oh, Daddy!" She leapt upon him. "It's the most wonderful, unexpected party I could have imagined!"

After a while, the whole party joined in singing happy birthday to her, most of them unsure what name to use in the song. "Who wants cake?" Angelica's mom said afterwards. She looked around for something to slice the cake with. "Oh! Just a moment, I forgot the knife," she said.

"No need!" the shirtless war veteran cried out. "I can cut it!" he said, raising his hook.

"Oh, please no!" her mother said. "I'll be right back."

Big D and his gang stayed by the food truck, laughing at everything they saw and eating one gourmet hot dog after another.

The old man wandered around, giving his opinion on everything. The black woman caught him stuffing food into his pockets, which were lined with ziplocks. "Mind your business!" he said. Then they both laughed.

The Chinese woman smiled and quietly clapped her hands as her daughter jumped in the bounce house with the perm lady's cats.

George did his best to avoid the woman from across the street, but eventually she cornered him by the dunking booth. He sipped his beer while she talked.

The first woman's seven children did the slip 'n slide so many times that the soap had run out and some of the waterspouts had broken. Nevertheless, they continued to slide. The bare plastic began to leave burns on their chests and chins, which they found hilarious and made into a contest.

Angelica basked in the weirdness of her party, until the most unexpected thing of all happened.

Three SUVs drove past the house, stopped suddenly, and reversed. The windows rolled down, revealing a number of gaping mouths. The cars turned off, and middle schoolers stepped slowly out of the cars. Heidi and Michael. Violet, Georgia and, most surprising of all, Tommy. Plus, another dozen classmates.

"Hey," Violet said, "I'm not grounded after all. Can I join?"

"Yeah," said Michael. "You're not so bad, Angelica, even if you are a mouth breather."

Angelica looked at all her classmates. Cool, handsome, beautiful, rich. She looked back at her weird party. Everyone had stopped what they were doing and were watching her.

"Sorry," she said, "You missed your chance. We're out of room. Plus," she shrugged, "This party's for misfits only."

"Ugh," Heidi said, "Are you turning me away just because I'm beautiful?"

"Yeah," Tommy said, "Is it so wrong to be cool?"

"No," Angelica said. "Not at all. I'm turning you away because you're not really my friends."

"These people aren't your friends either," Tommy said. "Do you even know all these freaks?"

"We're becoming friends. At least they came. Maybe if you weren't so cool and beautiful you would've been willing to come in the first place, willing to come to a party even for a weirdo like me." Her new friends came and stood beside her, looking at all the middle schoolers.

Finally, Violet said, "Whatever," and led the rest of the middle schoolers back into their vehicles.

"Now," Angelica said, turning and looking around at her new friends, "As you were."

Questions

1. Angelica is described as a misfit. How is that also an accurate description of Jesus, especially his earthly life?
2. How did Angelica's father go to "the highways and the hedges" to find party guests? What was the result?
3. How are the guests a picture of the kingdom? In what sense is being a "misfit" in this world a requirement (see Matt 5:3-12)?
4. Why did Angelica turn away her rich / beautiful / cool classmates? How does this reflect verses like Luke 14:11 and James 4:6?

The Parable of the Prodigal Son
Luke 15:11-32

"There was a man who had two sons. And the younger of them said to his father, 'Father, give me the share of property that is coming to me.' And he divided his property between them. Not many days later, the younger son gathered all he had and took a journey into a far country, and there he squandered his property in reckless living. And when he had spent everything, a severe famine arose in that country, and he began to be in need. So he went and hired himself out to one of the citizens of that country, who sent him into his fields to feed pigs. And he was longing to be fed with the pods that the pigs ate, and no one gave him anything.

"But when he came to himself, he said, 'How many of my father's hired servants have more than enough bread, but I perish here with hunger! I will arise and go to my father, and I will say to him, "Father, I have sinned against heaven and before you. I am no longer worthy to be called your son. Treat me as one of your hired servants."' And he arose and came to his father. But while he was still a long way off, his father saw him and felt compassion, and ran and embraced him and kissed him. And the son said to him, 'Father, I have sinned against heaven and before you. I am no longer worthy to be called your son.' But the father said to his servants, 'Bring quickly the best robe, and put it on him, and put a ring on his hand, and shoes on his feet. And bring the fattened calf and kill it, and let us eat and celebrate. For this my son was dead, and is alive again; he was lost, and is found.' And they began to celebrate.

"Now his older son was in the field, and as he came and drew near to the house, he heard music and dancing. And he called one of the servants and asked what these things meant. And he said to him,

'Your brother has come, and your father has killed the fattened calf, because he has received him back safe and sound.' But he was angry and refused to go in. His father came out and entreated him, but he answered his father, 'Look, these many years I have served you, and I never disobeyed your command, yet you never gave me a young goat, that I might celebrate with my friends. But when this son of yours came, who has devoured your property with prostitutes, you killed the fattened calf for him!' And he said to him, 'Son, you are always with me, and all that is mine is yours. It was fitting to celebrate and be glad, for this your brother was dead, and is alive; he was lost, and is found.'"

See also: *The Parables of the Lost Sheep & Lost Coin*

The Last Hurrah

"LET'S CELEBRATE," Sally had told him. "I'll meet you at the Last Hurrah."

Andy stepped into the bar and sat at their usual table near the window. She had not yet arrived, so he ordered a scotch and waited. Having just passed his dissertation, he was glad and full of hope, not only for his career, but because Sally had always said they'd marry once he finished school. He'd been waiting on this for many years, the moment when life was supposed to begin.

The clarinet jazz in the background brought back memories

of their first date, almost ten years ago, not too long after he had moved to Boston. 'Don't you just love this swanky place?' she had asked, running her hands on the leather lounge chair and looking up at the wood-paneled ceiling. She had teased him for not knowing the word 'swanky,' but he hadn't minded.

Stirring him from his memory, the waiter set his drink and a parlor dish of warm pecans on the table. Standing next to him, Andy noticed the waiter lingering. "Pardon me, are you Andrew Wyatt, by chance?"

"I am," Andy said, looking up.

"A young lady left a letter for you with the concierge."

Andy thanked the waiter and took the envelope and letter opener from the wooden serving tray. *To Andrew Wyatt, PhD* it said on the front. The back of the envelope was sealed with a literal kiss. He cut open the side to pull out the letter and a ring fell into his hand. The letter smelled of her perfume, like fresh flowers.

> *Andy,*
>   *I can't go through with it all. I just can't. I'm not who you think I am. Please, move on with your life. And don't wait on me, I'm not coming back. You deserve better anyway.*
>   *Forgive me (or don't),*
>   *Sally*
>   *PS: Congrats on your dissertation.*

If the waiter had by chance looked at Andy while he read the letter, he would have been surprised to have learned what it contained, for Andy showed no outward emotion toward it. He simply placed the envelope with the letter and ring in the chest pocket of his pea coat, swirled and smelled his scotch, and looked out at the lamplit, wintry streets of Boston. Now, Andy was, in fact, heartbroken. Deeply so. Yet, he refused to grieve. To grieve was to admit his loss. To grieve, in his mind, was to give her up. Instead, he swore an oath to himself that he would one day find and marry Sally Parker.

Every day since receiving the letter, he came back to the bar, ordered his drink, and waited for her. He would swirl and smell the scotch but would not drink it. He would place his hand on top of the parlor dish of nuts and feel the warmth but leave them uneaten. Then he'd take the letter from his jacket pocket, unfold it carefully, and read it. It still held her floral fragrance, which kept her alive in his memory and renewed his will. After reading it, he'd stare out the window, looking for her. He'd watch to see who got out of the taxi. He'd study the posture and stride of the tourists walking the Freedom Trail. He'd check the faces that entered the lobby of the Omni Parker hotel which housed the bar. Occasionally he would see someone who resembled her. Perhaps a beret similar to hers or the way a woman held a man's arm crossing the street or someone with her Norwegian blonde hair. But when the sighting proved false, as it always did, the initial thrill of it only added to the pain of his longing for Sally.

His friends from grad school or work would sometimes come with him. "Come on, Andy, drink up!"

"Not yet," he'd say.

Over time, the hotel and bar staff, observing him and overhearing his conversations, learned his story and became the most sympathetic, though quiet, supporters of his cause. They could see better than anyone the toll his waiting took on him and did their best to encourage him.

Now, almost three years later, Andy continued his evening routine. Patrick, his coworker and former roommate, had come with him this time. They sat and talked while Andy people watched, discussing the usual. Work projects. The Red Sox. The best seafood in town. The Bruins. Memories from grad school. The Red Sox.

When the conversation lulled, Patrick said, "So Andy. Let's talk about Sally."

Andy turned to him. "Sally? What about her?"

"Seen or heard from her since . . . you know, she left?"

"No, no one has."

"How long have you waited now?"

Andy shifted around uncomfortably in his chair. "It's been about three winters."

"Tried calling her?"

"She changed her number, you know that."

"You have any idea where she is?"

"No."

"Do you have any reason to believe she's coming back?"

Andy turned from the window and swirled his drink, raising its earthy odor. "She has given me no reason, if that's what you mean."

"Then please, tell me - and I'm sorry to put it this way - why have you sat here for three years like a lost kitten, waiting for her?"

"I'm not lost," Andy said.

"Call it what you want. You're pursuing the one girl in a hundred who wants nothing to do with you. It just makes no sense. You've got no reason to expect she'll return."

"I wouldn't say that."

"What?"

"That I've got no reason."

"You just said —"

"I said *she's* given me no reason."

Patrick stared at Andy. "Please, explain it to me so I know what to say the next time a woman asks about you at work."

"Patrick," Andy said, glancing at someone who had just entered the bar. "You of all people should understand."

Patrick waited for further explanation. "Why is that?"

"Because you're a professor of math. And at MIT of all places."

"I'm sorry," Patrick said, shaking his head. "The connection eludes me."

"I'll put it this way. Sixty plus years ago, MIT was approached for help with a special mission. A mission that, mathematically speaking, there were no known solutions for. A project fraught with problems and risks. A mission that many called, at best, impractical, and at worst, a setup for national embarrassment."

Andy stopped and let Patrick think while he watched the pedestrians cross Tremont. Finally, Patrick said, "Oh. You mean NASA?"

"Yes."

"Again, the connection between the moon landing and your unrequited love remains unclear to me."

"Some missions are worth embarking on, despite the odds and risks, simply because of what could be. That's all." Andy looked at Patrick, whose face was blank. "Let me try again," he said. "At work, there are some problems that you look at and, immediately, you know the answer, right?"

"Yes."

"But then there are others that you look at, and the answers don't come. You write it on the board and leave it there where you can stare at it. You attempt solutions, and when they don't work, you erase them and go home. The next day, what do you do? You try it from a different angle. And when it doesn't work, you sleep on it and try again. We can't all be Will Hunting, Patrick. After all, you worked on the same problem for years for your dissertation."

"Go on."

"Again, how long did it take Oppenheimer to split the atom? How long for Einstein to formulate the equivalence of mass and energy?"

"I don't know."

"A long time. Now, here's the real question. What do they all have in common? Einstein, Oppenheimer, Kennedy-era astrophysicists - what's the common denominator?"

"You got me, I don't know," Patrick said.

"They saw a seemingly unsolvable problem but had the will to work at it until it was resolved. Just like you on your white board. You see the problem and you know, you *know*, there's a solution. And you keep working at it until, one day, perhaps years later, something clicks, and it falls into place. That's the beautiful thing about math, right? All we're doing is discovering the order of the world, describing the way it all works. Numbering reality. Every problem has to have a solution."

"Ever tried to divide by zero?"

"That's not an unsolvable problem. That's a violation of the rules."

"You're crazy, you know that? You're wicked smart, but you're crazy. Sally is a human, a really cold-hearted human at that. She's not a math equation. You're going to die in this bar, a lonely old man who lived his whole life in denial, refusing to admit that his heart was broken."

"I will wholeheartedly admit to a broken heart. I'm just refusing to let it heal. You misunderstand me. My broken heart is the problem. And the solution is to find and marry Sally Parker. But, of course, knowing the solution is not the same as knowing the formula . . ." Andy looked down at the floor.

"You're dividing by zero, Andy. You need a shrink. Did you know when Alice heard about all this, she asked if you're on the spectrum?"

Andy shrugged and smiled. "Maybe I am."

"It's not funny. I'm serious about this," Patrick said, "You're waiting on someone who has obviously moved on and is probably married by now. Knowing Sally, she's probably been in the arms of a dozen men by now."

Andy winced. "I'm not just waiting, Patrick, I'm searching. Sally is lost, but I plan to find her."

"What, by moping around in this bar? And she's not lost, she left you."

"She left because she's lost. She's hiding, and all my will is bent upon finding her. I like to believe she hears me calling. That she knows I'm here, waiting on her somehow."

"What are you, Sauron?"

Andy smiled. "Something like that. Dark Lord or not, you've got to admire his devotion to the Ring."

Patrick put his head in his hands. "What are you going to do when you find her? Huh? How are you going to convince her to return to you? And even then, remain faithful?"

"The fact that I've waited for her will be all she needs. The lengths I've gone to find her will be sufficient for a change of heart. That's why I have to stay here and wait. If she were to return and I wasn't here looking for her, she would have no proof of my love for her. What was it Einstein allegedly said? 'Compound interest is the eighth wonder of the world.'"

"So essentially, your love is compounding interest as you wait on Sally."

"Exactly. The longer I go without giving up, the more I sacrifice, the more it will mean when I find her."

"What you mean is you're putting her in your debt the longer you wait on her. That sounds kind of twisted."

"Oh, no, just the opposite. I'm paying her debt." Andy shook his head and smiled. "An Ivy League education and yet you know so little of the human heart."

"Ok, I didn't want to do this to you." Patrick picked up his glass and took a sip. His face was red. He cleared his throat and reached in his pocket and pulled out his phone. After a moment, he handed it to Andy. It was a picture of Sally in a white dress with a headline underneath. *Sally Parker to wed Hugh Gaines, November 12.* "I'm sorry, Andy. Somebody sent this to me yesterday."

Andy swirled his scotch and smelled it. "Thank you for your friendship, I appreciate you telling me."

"I'm sorry, I really am. I figured it would take something like this for you to move on."

"I know, thank you. It's a blow, for sure." Andy picked up the letter and fanned himself with it briefly, its scent wafting towards him. "You misunderstand me, though. I'm not moving on. There is no other solution, Patrick."

"You realize November 12th was last Saturday."

"I realize that."

"She's married, man. It's over!"

"People divorce."

"Andy!" Patrick said, beginning to shout. "Come on, man! It's time. She has obviously moved on."

"But I haven't. I swore an oath to myself, did I ever tell you that? That I would find and marry her."

Patrick put his hands up in surrender. "OK, you win. I've gotta go."

"I'm sorry I've upset you."

"What upsets me is the thought of you wasting your life on a girl that left you high and dry. What about the rest of the people in your life? Your friends? Colleagues? What about me? If only you gave us a fraction of the time you've wasted searching for her. You won't even raise a glass with me."

"You're my best friend, Patrick. You're here. Why would I need to search for what is not lost? You could wait with me."

"Not a chance. What she did is so wrong, man. Honestly, I think she's evil. Every time I think about you waiting on her here - I'm sorry - I just hate her all the more, for *your* sake. Even if by some miracle she returned, would you really receive her back? Just like that?"

"It's called forgiveness. Or perhaps to use a term you could understand, dividing by zero." Patrick stood up. "Wait, please," Andy said. "Just a few more minutes. Finish your drink, at least."

"Fine." Patrick sat back down.

"Perhaps I am a fool. And I do grow old and withered, waiting here with an untouched scotch and a dish of cold pecans."

Patrick raised his eyebrows and nodded vigorously. "Exactly."

"Or - just humor me here - perhaps, by the slightest chance, by the same sliver of a chance that we learned to split the atom, you receive a call from me tomorrow. Or next year. Or twenty years from now. And you answer the phone and I say, 'Patrick, I found her.'" Andy paused. "I'm willing to give my life for that chance."

Patrick sighed. "You're a lunatic, you know that? Tell you what. If that happens, I'll meet you here, any day, any time, and we'll celebrate. Drinks on me."

"I look forward to it."

Patrick stood and put on his coat. "Maybe next time we should talk about the Red Sox instead of Sally."

"That'd be fine. See you next time." Patrick left the bar and headed south towards the Park Street T station. When Andy was sure he was gone, he reached up and touched his coat pocket that still held the ring. Suddenly overcome with weariness and pain, Andy covered his eyes with his hand and wept.

After some time, the waiter approached him. "Are you well, sir? Can I get you something?"

Andy wiped his eyes and looked up at him. "Thank you, Roger. I'll be fine soon enough."

The long New England winter descended on the city and, after many days, melted into spring. Spring bloomed into summer, then blushed into fall. Nothing. Andy continued to come each day after work and sit across from the empty chair with his drink. Although his resolve did not weaken nor his affections wander, with each passing season his longing grew increasingly painful. Patrick was not the last friend to try and convince Andy to move on. Some found his habit too sad to come around anymore. Some, too infuriating. Invariably, they thought he was a fool and grew tired of it all, drifting away. The staff of the hotel and bar, on the other hand, had become fond of him and encouraged him, in their own quiet way, in his search for Sally Parker.

The fifth winter since she'd left, Andy walked through the gold revolving doors into the Omni Parker hotel, and an old, familiar scent hit him like a stiff drink. *Sally?* he thought, scanning the room. But then he saw the porters in the lobby exchanging the day's floral centerpiece for a new one. *No.* Aching, he took a left into the bar and assumed his place.

He ordered the usual and looked out the window at the winter cityscape. The gray day had already turned to night. Dirty snowdrifts, steaming sewer grates, overly salted sidewalks. As he observed it all, he could have sworn he saw a woman walk by across the street with Sally's stride, but before it registered, she was gone. He turned and looked around at the people in the bar.

Some of the happy hour usuals. Several tourists. A few couples from the hotel.

The couple nearest him, discussing their plans for the week, brought back memories. He and Sally often came here after a long evening of study for a nightcap. 'Let's share a dessert,' she'd say, 'Your pick.' He wasn't much for sweets, but he liked to see her smile, so he'd order something for them to share. She always ate according to the weather. Crème brulée when it was cold. On warmer days, key lime pie. Rain or snow? Boston cream pie. They'd shared a lot of cream pies.

Stirring him out of his recollection, out of the corner of his eye, he caught a flash of blond hair, but it was gone by the time he turned his head. He stood and leaned his head against the cold glass, trying to look alongside the hotel. The streetlamps had come on now, casting a golden light on the snow. His heart raced, but after five minutes, settled back into a dull pain.

He reached for his drink to smell it but noticed he had not yet received it. He looked toward the bar and motioned to the waiter. The bartender was speaking with the concierge, who was glancing in his direction. *Everything is off tonight,* he thought. Finally, the waiter brought him his drink.

"Thank you, Roger," he said. The waiter lingered. "Something else?" Andy said, lifting his eyes.

Roger seemed nervous. "A letter for you." Andy took the envelope and letter opener from the wooden tray, and the waiter retreated to the bar, watching from afar.

Andy sliced open the side of the envelope. Fresh flowers. He closed his eyes, took a deep breath, and unfolded the note.

Andy,

I'm hardly worth the wait, you know. I ruined everything - your life, mine. Us. Yet here you are, after all these years. I don't get it. Let me make it up to you, somehow, and then I'll go.

Sally

Andy stood suddenly and looked around the room. He searched the street out the window. Then he glanced at the entrance to the bar and saw someone duck out. He jogged into the large, wood paneled lobby, looking towards the front desk and elevators. He was headed to the concierge to ask where the letter came from when he saw a woman push through the doors of the north entrance and run toward the taxi line.

Andy ran across the carpeted lobby, past the flower arrangement, and down the steps. Bursting through the doors into the snowy street, he leapt in front of the taxi line as the first cab began to drive away.

"Stop!" he cried, putting his hands on the hood of the car. The taxi stopped abruptly, the cabby cursing him. Andy leaned forward and peered through the icy windshield into the car to see who it was trying to hide in the back. *Sally.*

He came around to the passenger door and knocked gently on the windshield. She rolled it down but did not look at him.

"Found you," he said.

"I . . . I'm so sorry. I thought maybe I could . . ."

"Why can't you?" he said.

"I can't."

"Can't what? Sally, look at me."

"I can't face it all."

"Come inside. Let's talk about it."

"No, I'd better not."

The cab driver suddenly spoke up. "Hey listen, you two. Either go or don't. Yah wastin' my time."

Andy took five dollars from his wallet and handed it to the driver. Then he reached through the window and touched her cold hand. "Come inside."

Sally looked up at him, studying his face for a while. "Alright," she said finally. She got out and walked with him, stepping through the winter sludge and up the salted steps, back into the Omni Parker. A porter opened the door for them and nodded to Andy. As they went inside, the cabby stuck his head out the car window and yelled to the cab behind him. "You believe that guy?"

They sat in their spot next to the window. Sally kept on her light coat. Any time Andy looked at her she averted her eyes. He motioned to the waiter, who promptly approached them. "Drink for the miss?"

"Hot toddy, please," Andy said. The waiter nodded and walked to the bar. "Take your time," he said to Sally, who seemed restless. "It's good to see you."

The waiter brought the drink. She looked down at it and cupped her hands around it to warm them. "Here," he said. He took his pea coat off the back of his chair and put it around her shoulders. As he did so he noticed no rings on her fingers. He sat down across from her again and took a sip of his scotch.

"It's hard to know where to start," she said, taking a pecan from the dish. "You know, I haven't stepped foot in Boston since I left. I couldn't face it. I couldn't take the chance of running into you. I cut off everyone. I mean *everyone*."

"And yet, you're here."

"Enough time passed and I thought, maybe a visit would be therapeutic. Put the past to bed, you know? Start over. I had a good life here. I figured everyone had moved on, maybe it was safe again. I got here this morning and have been walking around the city all day, trying to make peace with it. And then . . . and then, half an hour ago, I was walking up Beacon, cold as death, and I saw the bar at the corner, glowing almost. I thought, 'Maybe I'll step in for a warm drink. For old time's sake.' And when I came through the revolving doors, what did I see? Andrew Wyatt - so close I could reach out and touch him. I panicked and just circled right back outside."

"And yet, you're here."

"I watched you through the window for a bit, looking over your shoulder. You just sat there, sitting in the same old spot, *our* spot. I stood there freezing and waiting to see who you were meeting. At first it wasn't much more than morbid curiosity. I could tell you were looking for someone. After a while the most bizarre thought hit me, *What if he's waiting for me?* I kept watching, fighting against the thought. *No, don't be such a narcissist,* I told myself. *That was five years ago, of course he's moved on. You're the last person he'd want to see.* I got desperate for someone, *anyone,* to come and sit down with you. But no one came."

Sally took a deep breath and continued. "I wasn't ready to face you, but I couldn't bear the thought any longer, so I came inside and asked the concierge for some paper and an envelope. I said, 'I need you to deliver a note to a man in the bar.' The concierge's eyes kind of lit up when I said that. She said, 'Is it for Dr. Wyatt, by chance?' I froze. She looked me up and down and didn't seem too pleased with me, and then she got the funniest look on her face. She said, 'You're her, aren't you? You're the one he's been waiting for all these years.' I could have *died* when she said that. I just wanted to run and hide."

"But you didn't."

"Well, not at first. When she said that I knew I couldn't leave without giving you an explanation. Maybe make amends so we could both move on with our lives. I figured you deserved at least that much."

"Then why'd you run?"

"I thought the letter might break the ice, and then I could face you. But when I looked in and saw your face as you read it, I realized it was all wrong. I couldn't bear for you to see me. Even now, I can hardly look you in the eye." She stirred the stick of cinnamon in her drink.

"What are you so ashamed of?"

"What kind of question is that? All of it, Andy. All I've put you through. And it's so much worse seeing you here waiting on me." She paused and looked down. "When we were together, I wasn't who you thought I was. I had another life. Secrets. Things I thought I could keep from you."

He noticed her hand shaking. "Have you eaten?"

"I'm fine," she said.

He motioned to the waiter, who approached him immediately. "Sir?"

"A bowl of chowder for the lady, please." She looked down at the word *lady*.

"I'll have someone bring it right over from the restaurant."

"Thank you, Roger."

During the few minutes of waiting neither of them said anything. Andy didn't want to rush her. He reached over and drew casually in the condensation on the windows. The soup came and she blew on it and sipped it from the spoon. "I guess I'm hungrier than I realized." She took another bite. "Famished, really."

"Keep going, Sally. I'm listening."

She opened the package of oyster crackers and dumped them into her soup. "Andy, while we were together - not the whole time - but, here and there, I had . . . there were . . ."

"Other men," he said. She looked up to see his face when he said it.

"Yes, that's right." She pushed the crackers around in her soup with the spoon. "I always felt you were too good for me, you know? The longer we were together, the more I felt that way. I swear, you're a *saint*. You were always such a gentleman. And I'm . . . I'm no lady. I have another side to me that I never let you know. I gave into it when I was away from you." She closed her eyes for a moment. "I always chose the sleaziest guys . . . because that's what I felt like I deserved." She shrugged. "Someone like me, I guess."

"I thought I could get away with it, and I did in a sense. But it turns out even I have a conscience, and it felt like it was tearing in two. I wanted to marry you - I did - but I had already proven that, well, let's just say fidelity is not a virtue of mine. So, when you finished school, and I no longer had a reason to delay the wedding, I had to leave. I ran off with one of them. I didn't love him, but . . . he was fun." She shrugged again. "He was moving to New York and said I could come along."

"Was he the one you married?"

She laughed. "No, he wasn't that type. Hugh - the one I did marry - he wasn't a dirtbag like all the rest. He was of a different sort. He knew about my past when we married, but thought he could control me, that he could *make me* faithful to him, you know what I mean? He tried to make a slave out of me. And I think I made a monster of him. It got dangerous. NYPD kept getting involved. The turning point came the last time he hit me. I realized I was hoping he would kill me, just finish me off. I actually wanted him to kill me. And he probably would have if the cops hadn't showed up and taken him. I didn't bail him out that time. Instead, I finally came to my senses and thought, 'What am I *doing* here?' And I left. It lasted less than a year. I've been a rolling stone ever since, trying to figure out where things went wrong. That's why I really came back to Boston, back to where life began to unravel. I had it good here. I thought maybe I could patch up things here and then start over." She shook her head. "And apparently the fates wanted me to begin by making amends with you." She put her spoon down next to her bowl. "So, tell me. How do I make it up to you?"

"There's no need."

"I need to."

"That's not what you need. Sally —"

"Stop."

"What?"

"I know what you're about to say," she said. "You misunderstand me. I just want to give you an explanation and make amends so I can move on. I wouldn't dare ask for forgiveness."

"You don't have to. You already have it."

"I can't receive it."

"Can't or won't?"

"What's the difference?"

"You can learn."

"No, God, Andy. Quit ordering me drinks and food and just throw it all in my face, will you? For crying out loud, hit me! Curse me. Turn me out into the streets. I had always been afraid that's what you'd do if I saw you - murder me or something. But this is much worse. I wish you hadn't followed me to the taxi. You should have left me out in the cold."

Andy looked out the window into the night. "You can go if you want. But just know, I'll be here, waiting. Another five, ten years. Whatever."

"But *why?*"

"Sally, look at me," he said. She looked him in the eye. "You know the answer to that."

"How can you *possibly* not hate me?"

"I may not be able to explain that to you."

"But I'm not worthy."

"I don't care. It's not about that."

"I'll make it up to you."

"There is nothing to make up. The past is forgotten."

She sighed and went back to her soup. After a few minutes of silence, she wiped the corners of her mouth with the napkin and said, "Listen, Andy. I understand why you've waited. You want to pick up where we left off, right?" He smiled and drained the rest of his scotch. "You're insane. You know that, right? Incredibly kind, but also - there's no other way to put it - clinically insane. A relationship is out of the question, and *certainly* a monogamous marriage. Even if my conscience could bear it, I've proven too many times that I'm incapable of faithfulness."

"I don't want to pick up where we left off."

"Oh?" She looked surprised and, Andy thought, a little disappointed. "Well, then what?"

"I want to start over. And this time, I want to know you as you really are. You'd be surprised what would happen if you'd let me love the real Sally. You never know, fidelity might start to come naturally."

She gave a wry smile. "Hugh already tried that. It didn't work."

"No, I don't think he did. He tried to control you. Faithfulness can't be forced, it has to be won - by things like patience, grace, and, if necessary, suffering. I'm not like Hugh. I'm not going to enslave you, Sally Parker, I'm going to woo you."

Her eyes grew moist and red. "What if it doesn't work? What if I'm too . . . what if I've ruined myself for good?"

"We wouldn't be having a conversation like this if you were ruined for good. As for winning your heart, it will take time, but leave that up to me."

"Then what do you want from me?"

"Just stay and talk with me for a while." He called the waiter over. "Can we get a crème brulée?" The waiter nodded, took her empty bowl and walked away.

Sally sat back in her chair and let out a deep sigh. Finally, the tension left her face and she smiled a little. "Alright," she said.

At midnight, having spent the evening together, Andy helped her with her coat and called her a taxi. She held his arm to keep from slipping on the ice. As he opened the door to the cab, Sally paused and looked up at him. "See you tomorrow?"

"You know where to find me."

She kissed him on the cheek and got into the cab, staring out the back window as it drove off. Andy turned around to find the hotel staff all gathered at the window behind him, cheering and waving him inside for a celebratory drink. He laughed and headed into the hotel. On his way up the steps, he took out his phone and made a call.

"Hello?" a weary voice said.

"Patrick?"

"Andy? It's like midnight, man."

"I know, I just wanted to let you know. I found her."

"What? Her who?"

"Sally."

"..."

"Come on, let's celebrate. Just like you said."

"Celebrate? All these years, you've refused to share a drink with me, but she shows up and now you're ready to party."

"Drink or not, you've always had my friendship. Besides, is it not fitting to celebrate?"

"Andy, even if by some microscopic chance you're not hallucinating, and this is real, I wouldn't step *foot* in a bar to celebrate that Jezebel. She's evil, man. I've told you before.

You're dealing with a seductress. A straight up *femme fatale*. If you have any self-respect, any sense of honor, don't take her back. There's no telling what she's after."

"I'm sorry you feel that way Patrick, that you can't share in my joy. If you change your mind, meet me at The Last Hurrah. Otherwise, have a good night, my friend."

The bar erupted in cheers when Andy came inside and crossed the threshold. He couldn't stop smiling, for the long winter of his waiting had come to an end, and life could begin again. The front desk workers and porters took turns shaking his hand. The bartender popped a bottle of champagne and filled their glasses, unconcerned as it overflowed onto the floor. The waiter passed out the glasses and the concierge cried out, "To Andy!" After they toasted him, Andy stood on a lounge chair, raised his glass and said with a wide smile, "To Sally, who was lost, and now is found."

Questions

1. How does Andy resemble the prodigal son's father? What qualities are especially magnified in Andy? What about Christ does this reflect?
2. How do you see the prodigal son in Sally?
3. In the parable, the son is given a ring, sandals, and a robe. Likewise, how does Andy diffuse Sally's guilt and shame when she returns?
4. Why did Sally not want to receive forgiveness, but to "make it up" to him? Why is this important?
5. What does Andy say will cause Sally to be faithful to him? How does this reflect biblical truth?
6. Andy says his aim is to woo Sally, not to control her. And he says it will take time. How is this similar to the way Jesus loves us?
7. Describe the difference between Patrick and the hotel and bar staff. What does Patrick not understand? How is this relevant to the parable?

PART 2

PARABLES OF WISDOM

The Parable of the Good Samaritan
Luke 10:25-37

And behold, a lawyer stood up to put him to the test, saying, "Teacher, what shall I do to inherit eternal life?" He said to him, "What is written in the Law? How do you read it?" And he answered, "You shall love the Lord your God with all your heart and with all your soul and with all your strength and with all your mind, and your neighbor as yourself." And he said to him, "You have answered correctly; do this, and you will live."

But he, desiring to justify himself, said to Jesus, "And who is my neighbor?" Jesus replied, "A man was going down from Jerusalem to Jericho, and he fell among robbers, who stripped him and beat him and departed, leaving him half dead. Now by chance a priest was going down that road, and when he saw him he passed by on the other side. So likewise a Levite, when he came to the place and saw him, passed by on the other side. But a Samaritan, as he journeyed, came to where he was, and when he saw him, he had compassion. He went to him and bound up his wounds, pouring on oil and wine. Then he set him on his own animal and brought him to an inn and took care of him. And the next day he took out two denarii and gave them to the innkeeper, saying, 'Take care of him, and whatever more you spend, I will repay you when I come back.' Which of these three, do you think, proved to be a neighbor to the man who fell among the robbers?" He said, "The one who showed him mercy." And Jesus said to him, "You go, and do likewise."

Bonita Juanita

Juanita sat on the bench at the bus stop, her hands resting on top of her stomach. She winced at a sudden, sharp pain. When it passed she thought, *I remember when things weren't like this.* As she waited her thoughts drifted back to her childhood in Oaxaca. She remembered the sound of her mother grinding corn. *Bonita Juanita*, her father used to call her.

The bus wheezed abruptly to a halt in front of her. One hand under her belly, one pushing up from the bench, she stepped carefully onto the bus. Reaching into her purse, she looked around for the fare. She was still not used to American coins. After she finally paid, the bus lurched forward before she had time to sit down. She caught herself from falling and quickly got into a seat, a pain radiating down her inner thighs.

She stared out the window, thinking of her father, who had disappeared in Tijuana. *Why did they take you away, Papi? Did you ask too many questions?* She turned to her last happy memory before everything went wrong, to her quinceañera three years ago, the celebration of her entrance to womanhood. *Palomita,* her mother had said, holding her face, *you are a woman now.*

At the next stop a handful of people shuffled off and on the bus. One of the new passengers, a man with a patchy beard and cutoff sleeves, scanned the seating options. Although there were plenty of empty spots, he came and sat next to her, bringing with him a scent of cigarettes and motor oil. He looked over at her and lifted his chin. She nodded and looked out the window, trying to edge away from the man without him noticing.

"You ain't gotta be scared," he said.

"Thank you," she said, a little short of breath. She felt around for her purse and drew it close to her. They rode for several minutes without speaking.

"When's it comin'?" he asked finally.

"What?"

"The baby," he said, gesturing towards her stomach.

She hesitated. "Still a few months away."

"Baby got a name?" he said.

"No."

"Baby got a daddy?" he said.

"No, not really."

"You scared? About the baby, I mean."

She looked over at him for a moment. "Yes," she said quietly. "Very much."

"Name's Kyle," he said, reaching out to shake her hand. "Listen, I got four kids. Ain't been prepared for a single one of 'em. You'll be alright," he said. "Ever'body gets scared."

"Thank you."

"I became a daddy when I was seventeen. You 'bout seventeen?"

"Eighteen."

"You from California? Or —"

"Mexico."

"Purty good English, *señorita*," he said. "Almost good as mine," he said, smiling at her, revealing a few missing teeth. "Way better than my *Español.*"

"Thank you," she said. "We spoke both in my home."

"When my girl's parents found out, she got kicked outta her house 'cause she wouldn't get rid of the baby. She came and lived with me and my daddy. She was scared. And mad as all get out. I was scared, too. Yes sir, yes sir. Dropped out of school an' started lookin' for a job. We got hitched and made it work somehow."

Juanita turned suddenly to him. "Why did she keep the baby?"

"Huh? Oh. Well now, lemme think." He stared ahead for a bit and then turned back to Juanita. "I ain't ever ask her that. Tell you what. I'll ask her when I get home. If I ever see you again, I'll let you know what she says."

"Alright. Thank you, Mr. Kyle."

"Aw, ain't no mister." He stood up. "Well, this is my stop. Gotta pickup my truck, been in the shop. Hey, you got a name?"

"Juanita."

"*Hasta la vista*, Juanita."

Juanita got off at the next stop and looked around. In front of her were a row of boarded up duplexes, behind her a 24 hour laundromat. A man sat on the curb not far from her, watching her. She looked at the address she had written down and started walking. After a few blocks, she turned a corner and walked inside the Southside Women's Clinic.

The lady at the front desk handed her a clipboard with paperwork. She filled it out, trying not to think too much about it. She handed it back to the lady, who flipped through it rapidly.

"Insurance?"

"No, no ma'am. I was told —"

"Fill this out, please." Juanita filled out the additional forms.

"It's five hundred upfront," the lady said. "We'll send you a bill for the second half after the procedure." Juanita reached into her purse and took out the money, counting it several times before handing it to the lady.

After half an hour someone opened a door and called her back, where she sat in another room, waiting. Finally, a nurse in green scrubs came in with a clipboard.

"How far along are you?" the nurse asked without looking at her.

"Near the end of the second trimester, I think. I'm not sure."

"That's pretty far along. It would've been easier for you if you'd come sooner."

"Yes, I know."

"You should have come sooner."

"I know."

"And you forgot to put your PCP on your paperwork."

"PCP?" Juanita said.

"Your primary care physician."

"I don't have one."

The nurse said something under her breath and wrote in her notes. "Looks like you're unmarried?"

"Yes."

She flipped through some papers on her clipboard and then

turned toward the door. "Come with me," she said. They proceeded down the hall to a dimly lit room. "Lie down and lift your dress," she said. Juanita lifted it to her waist. "This is an ultrasound, I need to see your stomach." The lady applied the gel to her stomach and moved the device around on her, tapping keys on her computer every once in a while.

Juanita knew what was on the screen and tried to find other objects around the room to hold her focus. *Mami, how has it come to this?*

"You're not in your second trimester."

"Oh?" Juanita said, wiping her eyes.

For the first time, the nurse looked at Juanita tenderly. "You're almost full-term," she said quietly, "There's nothing we can do, Juanita."

"What?" Juanita said, "No, but I can't do this!"

"I'm sorry, once there's fetal viability it's not legal."

"Please!" Juanita said, turning to beg the woman. And when she did, she saw what was on the screen that she had been trying to avoid. *Ay! Papi, tu nieto!* She brushed the nurse's hand away, wiped her stomach with the paper towels and pulled down her dress. "I need to go. *Santa Maria Madre de Dios,*" Juanita said, crossing herself. "*Ayúdeme!*" She stood and reached for the door.

The nurse grabbed her wrist from across the bed. "Juanita."

"Yes?" she said, looking over her shoulder, feeling like the walls of the windowless room were closing in on her.

"It's a girl."

Juanita closed the door behind her, her hands shaking. She walked down the hall and felt her abdomen tighten suddenly. She leaned on the wall, closed her eyes, and tried to breathe. When it passed, she approached the front desk and waited until the lady looked up at her. "I've decided not to go through with the procedure," she said. "May I have the money back, please?"

The woman laughed. "Honey, didn't you read the paperwork? It says 'Nonrefundable Deposit.' Do you know what that means? Or do you need it translated?"

"I know what that means."

"Well?"

"I was hoping you might make an exception. I did not even meet with the doctor."

"I don't care if all you did was take a sip from the water fountain. Once you hand over the cash, it's gone. *Adios.* You were only paying a fraction in the first place. If you keep wasting my time I'm going to bill you for the other half."

Juanita stared at her and began to tremble. "That was everything I had."

"Not my *problemo.*"

"I was hoping you might . . . have mercy."

"You're in America now. It doesn't work like that." She looked over Juanita's shoulder and said, "Next!"

Juanita turned around slowly and walked out the door. She stood outside, shielding her eyes from the bright sunlight, and a woman approached her. "Hello," the woman said. She handed Juanita a pamphlet. "I'm a volunteer with Samaritan Crisis Pregnancy Clinic. Do you have a moment to talk?"

"Yes, alright."

"If you are interested in another option for your baby, we offer comprehensive services. Tests and ultrasounds, counseling and parent education courses. Even prenatal care and financial support for the birth."

"That sounds very nice." She paused. "But I just spent everything I have."

"No, that's the best part - it's all free!"

"Oh, how wonderful."

"Yes, and we're located just around the corner. I can walk with you if you want to go there now?"

"Sure, thank you."

They walked a few blocks and made a turn until they arrived at the clinic. The lady stopped at the steps leading to the front door. "Alright, God bless!" she said, walking back.

Juanita stepped slowly into the building and was greeted warmly by a lady at the front desk.

"Hello, I am interested in your services the lady told me about. I'm coming from the Southside Women's Clinic."

"Oh, yes. Just fill out this paperwork and we'll be right with you."

Juanita filled it out and handed it back to the woman. After a few minutes the woman called her to the desk.

"You didn't provide a social security number."

"No, ma'am."

"Do you have one?"

"No, I don't."

"So, you're not a US citizen."

"That's correct. I was born in Oaxaca." The lady looked confused. "Mexico."

The lady nodded. "Do you have a visa?"

"No ma'am."

"Green card?"

"No ma'am."

"Any immigration documentation at all?"

Juanita looked down, silent.

The lady clucked her tongue. "Well, that's going to limit what services we can offer you." She pointed to a sign pinned to the wall behind her. It said, in English and Spanish, "UNDOCUMENTED? SERVICES LIMITED TO PREGNANCY TESTS AND PRENATAL LITERATURE."

The lady handed her a paper bag with some items in it. "We have to prioritize care or else we'd penalize those who are here legally. It would stretch us too thin to take on everybody."

"Please," Juanita said, "Have mercy."

"Sorry, it's not my decision. It's a donor thing. The ones who keep the lights on here have certain rules about how the money is used."

Juanita took the paper bag and walked outside. She sat down on the concrete steps. *Abuela, only yesterday I played at your feet.* She would have cried but her abdomen began to squeeze itself again. "Ay!" she said, bending forward.

When the sensation passed, Juanita stood from the steps and began walking back to the bus stop. When she got to the main road and was about to sit down on the bench, she realized she didn't have enough for the fare back home. The man was still there on the curb, looking at her. She considered asking him for the money but didn't think she could take another rejection that day.

Juanita began to walk alongside the street in the heat and dust and diesel fumes. Her watch showed 1:00pm. She was supposed to clean a house starting at 2:30 and was trying to think how to get there from this part of town. Stopping at a 7/11, she asked for directions. The cashier told her the neighborhood she was looking for was about five miles west. "Thank you, sir," she said. She lingered in the cool of the store for a few minutes, slowly walking the aisles. Opening a door to one of the coolers, she rested her hand on a glass Coca-Cola bottle and sighed. She walked back outside.

"Ay!" the pain came again after a few minutes of walking. She bent forward and put her hands on her knees and closed her eyes. It took longer to go away this time. *Papi, give me your hand.*

She stood and continued walking down the main road. Passing a hot dog stand, she realized she had not eaten since she left her apartment that morning. Even so, her thirst was worse than her hunger. She regretted not sipping from the water fountain at the clinic. A few minutes later, outside a shop she saw a spigot with a hose coiled beneath it for watering plants. When she was sure no one in the store was looking, she turned it on and drank the warm water before continuing her westward walk.

Twice in fifteen minutes Juanita had to stop and breathe through the pain in her abdomen and thighs. She began to understand what was happening. She thought about going back to the clinic, about going through with the procedure. *I can't do this, Mami, I am not the woman you said I am.* She looked around wildly as she walked, looking for some kind of escape. About ten minutes later, when the pains began to come again, she stepped aside into a parking lot and squatted down in the shade of a tree. As she did so, a burst of fluid ran down her legs and onto the ground. Juanita was alarmed, but in too much pain to speak. When the pain finally passed she tried to stand, but now felt a different pain. Any movement at all made her insides feel like fire. She leaned against the bark of the tree and closed her eyes. Juanita thought of the mango tree in Oaxaca she used to read beneath after school. *Come inside, Bonita Juanita, it is time to eat. Your mother has been looking for you.*

"I can't. Tell *Mami* I cannot do it. I'm sorry, I am so very sorry. I think I am dying," she said. "*Lo siento, mi Papi, tengo miedo.*"

"You ain't gotta be scared," a voice said.

Juanita opened her eyes. Patchy beard. Cutoff sleeves.

"The baby's comin', ain't it?" Kyle said.

Juanita nodded.

"You need a ride?"

She nodded. "Hospital."

"All right, let's go."

"I can't walk," she said.

"I can carry you if that's alright."

She nodded. He went and opened the rear door of his rusted truck, shoving things off the seat to the floor. He knelt beside Juanita.

"I ... I'm wet. I'm so sorry," she said.

"I know, it's alright. Ain't my first rodeo. I'll be easy and gentle." He put an arm around her back and under her legs and picked her up. As he carried her to the truck, she smelled the motor oil and cigarettes again, but now that she was closer, there was another scent. Something she couldn't place, something that reminded her of home. He placed her carefully on the back seat and closed the door. When he sat in the driver's seat, he turned the mirror towards her and said, "I'll drive best I can, but it ain't gon' feel too good." The engine turned over a few times and started. "Which hospital's your doc at?"

"I don't have a doctor. Wherever's closest."

"No doc, huh? You got any insurance? Medicaid?"

"No."

"*Señorita*, if you have that baby at the hospital they'll rob you blind. I don't care what they say. Seen it happen too many times. Tell you what, just come on to my house. My wife — she birthed four babies at home by herself. Helped all the neighbors birth their babies, too."

"Please, just go," Juanita said, another pain coming.

"Alright, *vamanos*," he said. "Plus, you'll have a chance to ask her why she kept 'em." He paused. "S'pose it don't matter much at this point." Despite Kyle's careful driving, the ride was agonizing. She couldn't help but moan. "Hang on, Juanita. Almost there."

Finally, they pulled into a wooded trailer park. Kyle parked next to one of the trailers and got out. He was about to pick up Juanita but realized she was in the grip of a pain. "*Mamita!*" he shouted over the truck. Several dogs came and started barking and jumping toward Kyle. "Go on, get!" he said. "*Mamita!* Get out here, woman! *Ayúdeme!*" he cried toward the trailer. When he saw the pain had passed, he picked up Juanita. "Easy now," he said. As he brought her near the house, a hispanic woman who looked hardly older than Juanita came out the door, holding an infant. She looked angry until she saw Juanita.

"We got a baby comin'. Quick!" Kyle said. Two young children leapt off a tire swing behind the trailer, trying to see who he was carrying.

"Put her on the bed," the woman said with a thick accent. "I need hot water. Towels, rags. Then take the children and go. *Andele!*"

Kyle placed Juanita on his bed. "She's gon' take real good care of you, Juanita. You ain't gotta be scared. You'll be alright." He gathered the children and went out the screen door.

Kyle returned late that night. He left the children in the car and came to the door, opening it cautiously, listening. "Hello?" he called into the house. "*Mamita?*"

"Shhh! In here. Come."

Kyle walked into his bedroom. Juanita sat up against the headboard, her eyes closed. Laying on her chest, swaddled in a dish towel, was a little brown, waxy baby, asleep. *Mamita* sat in a chair in the corner, folding laundry.

"It go OK?" he said quietly.

"Yes, *muy bien.*"

"Boy or girl?"

"*Niña,*" *Mamita* said, tossing a pair of socks into a basket.

"She got a name?" he said.

"Not yet."

"They might need somewhere to stay for a while," he whispered. "Might need some help. She don't have nobody."

"Of course," *Mamita* said. "She can have our room." Kyle nodded.

"*Mercedes,*" Juanita said, without opening her eyes. Kyle and *Mamita* looked over at the mother and child. "Her name is *Mercedes.*"

Kyle turned to *Mamita,* bewildered. He leaned toward her.

"She named her after a car?" he whispered.

Mamita threw a towel at him. "*Burro!*"

The bed began to shake slightly. They looked over at Juanita, who had raised a hand to her eyes. *Mamita* cast a murderous glance at Kyle, thinking he'd upset her. But then Juanita dropped her hand, and they saw that she was not crying but, for the first time since her quinceañera, laughing again like a little girl.

Questions

1. How was Juanita, like the parable, "left half dead"? Similarly, in what ways was her plea for mercy denied?

2. Did you feel compassion for Juanita? Why or why not?

3. In what ways did this story surprise you? How is that similar to the surprises in the parable?

4. What prompted Jesus to tell this parable, and why is that important?

5. How does this story / parable redefine "neighbor?"

6. Why did Juanita gave her baby its name?

7. How did the mercy Juanita received change her at the end?

Subversive Stories

The Parable of the Friend at Midnight
Luke 11:1-8

Now Jesus was praying in a certain place, and when he finished, one of his disciples said to him, "Lord, teach us to pray, as John taught his disciples." And he said to them, "When you pray, say:
> "Father, hallowed be your name.
> Your kingdom come.
> Give us each day our daily bread,
> and forgive us our sins,
> for we ourselves forgive everyone who is indebted to us.
> And lead us not into temptation."

And he said to them, "Which of you who has a friend will go to him at midnight and say to him, 'Friend, lend me three loaves, for a friend of mine has arrived on a journey, and I have nothing to set before him'; and he will answer from within, 'Do not bother me; the door is now shut, and my children are with me in bed. I cannot get up and give you anything'? I tell you, though he will not get up and give him anything because he is his friend, yet because of his impudence he will rise and give him whatever he needs."

See also: *The Parable of the Persistent Widow*

Habibi

"Ah, my friend, my friend," Abdulhadi said, knocking on the glass door as he entered my office.

"Good to see you, friend," I said.

"Peace be to you, brother Yusuf," Abdulhadi said, saying my name in his native Arabic. He grabbed my hand and shook it, smiling.

"And to you."

"How are you?" he said.

"I am well, how are you, Abdulhadi?"

"I am well, praise God, brother," he said. "And how is your family?" he continued shaking my hand.

"We are well, thank you." He stared at me for a moment, clearly waiting for something. "Ah, and how is your family?"

"*Habibi*, we are at peace, thanks be to the God of Abraham, Isaac, and Jacob, whose mercy is forever, whose compassion is great."

"Yes," I said.

"... whose steadfast love reaches to the heavens ..."

"Uh-huh."

". . . and his faithfulness to the skies . . ."

"All right," I said. He finally released my hand but continued to smile. When he didn't say anything else, I said, "Abdulhadi, did you have something for me?"

"Eh? Ah, yes, of course, brother." He went into the hallway and brought in several packages.

We had hired Abdulhadi a few months prior as a supply runner. He had just arrived in the US as a refugee. In his interview, Abdulhadi shared stories of persecution as an Iraqi Christian and war stories of his time as a translator for the American Army. I think he knew I was the reason he got the job, because his first day at work he came and found me in the break room. Bowing his head again and again, he handed me a bag of oranges in front of everyone and said, "I am grateful to find the hospitality of a Christian brother in such a place. God's peace to you, *habibi.*"

Now in my office, after neatly stacking the packages in front of my desk, he lingered. I looked up from my computer. "Yes, Abdulhadi?"

"One question, brother. My wife, she has a virus on her computer. You are Chief Information Officer, no?" He raised his eyebrows. "In your wisdom, what do you recommend?"

"Well, I haven't worked on that kind of thing in a long time. You may want to ask the helpdesk down the hall."

"Yes, yes, of course," he said, disappearing from my office.

I got up from my seat, closed the glass door that he had left open, and returned to my work. Several minutes later, Abdulhadi knocked and entered my office again.

"Yes?"

"Ah, my friend Yusuf."

I looked at him, trying to be patient. "Yes?"

"They thought maybe it is the ransomware. They recommended a software. Tonight I will download it from the internet and install it, and it will clean the virus."

"That's great."

"Yes, thank you once again for your kindness, brother."

"No problem, have a nice day."

"Peace be unto you and your family," he said.

"Yes, same to you."

The next morning I came to work early to prepare for a board meeting later that day. When I arrived, my office door was unlocked. I looked through the glass and saw Abdulhadi standing inside my office with a woman.

"Ah, my friend, my friend," he said, a large smile on his face.

I looked at him for a moment. "Morning," I said.

"How are you?"

"A bit stressed. A lot of work to get done. You?" I set my things down on the desk.

"I am well," he said, "Thanks be to the God of Abraham, Isaac, and Jacob, who —"

"Abdulhadi, how did you get into my office?"

"I have keys, of course." His smile dropped at the look of frustration on my face. "Brother Yusuf, have I offended you?"

"The keys are for delivering packages, Abdulhadi. Is that why you are here?"

"No, *habibi*. This is my wife. She is called Noor. My

apologies, her English is not good."

"Hi, I'm Joe," I said, shaking the hand of the woman. She smiled and nodded but didn't say anything.

"Did you sleep well, brother?"

"I slept fine. Listen, I'm very busy. Do you need something?"

"Ah, yes, all right. The virus. I tried to install the software from the internet, but I was not successful."

"I'm sorry to hear that."

"I thought maybe you could take a look, brother." He motioned to his wife, who drew an old, large laptop from a bag. He put it on my desk and opened it. I did not say anything immediately, trying somehow to respond without anger. "Let's see," he said to himself. "Corporate wi-fi ... here it is ... ah yes, the password ..."

"Abdulhadi!" I shouted.

"Yes, brother?" he said, a look of surprise on both their faces.

"You can't connect an infected laptop to our network."

"Ah?"

"You'll infect the whole company!"

"Oh! My friend, yes, of course. It is a virus, no?" He closed the laptop and slipped it back into the bag.

"I'm sorry, I cannot help you with it here in the office. It is too dangerous. Besides, our department works on company computers only. That sort of thing has to be done at home."

"Ah, I am a fool, forgive me. Thank you for understanding."

"Yes, no problem. You didn't know."

He said something to his wife in Arabic. "Ah, *shukran,*" she said, smiling. He bowed and shook my hand. Both of them walked backwards out of my office, bowing again and smiling. Relieved, I began to prepare for my board meeting.

The next morning, a Saturday, I was looking forward to a long, slow morning in the privacy of my home. It was still dark outside when I woke, put on my robe, and went downstairs, intentionally leaving my phone in the bedroom. It would likely be another hour before my wife awoke and several more for my children. I sat down with a cup of coffee and rubbed my temples, still aching from the week of work. I sighed. *Finally.*

A knock at the door.

I took a sip of coffee. It was nothing.

Another, extended, knock at the door, which I could not deny.

Unbelievable. That solar panel salesman is at my house again - at 5:30am! Utterly shameless. I was angry but committed to ignoring him. *I swear, if he wakes up my kids . . .*

The knocks came three times more, about a minute apart. I turned on the news to block them out. After a while, the knocking stopped. When I was sure the salesman was gone, I turned the news off and sat in the quiet, trying to regain my moment of peace.

A shadow passed behind the curtains.

A knock at the backdoor.

I jumped out of the chair and charged forward. I unlocked the door and swung it open, ready to destroy the salesman.

"Ah, my friend, my friend!"

I stepped back in astonishment.

"How are you, brother?" he said. "You are awake, yes?"

I had no words.

Abdulhadi and his wife took their shoes off next to the door and came inside. They sat themselves down at my breakfast table, a bag beside them. I still stood at the door in shock.

"Abdulhadi," I said slowly.

"Yes, brother Yusuf?" he said, looking up at me and smiling.

"This is my house," I said.

"Ah, yes, yes I know. Beautiful! So clean. The God of Abraham has blessed you richly. *Mabruk,* as we would say."

"Where did you get my address?"

"Ah, of course. I meant to ask for it yesterday, but you were in your meeting, so I found it in the company postage system."

I squeezed the bridge of my nose. "It's not even 6am."

"Yes, the sun will be rising soon, if God wills it."

"This is not even remotely appropriate."

"Oh! My God, of course," he spoke tersely to his wife in Arabic. "Forgive me, brother." Embarrassed, she nodded and reached in her bag and handed me a package of dates and a decorative ceramic dish with a lid. "You know this treat? In my country we call it *baqlawa.*"

I took the food and put it on the table. I went to get the coffee pot and think for a moment. When I came to the table to fill my cup he said, "Ah! Yes! Coffee is perfect. No sugar for us though, the *baqlawa* is very sweet." I stared at him, the pot in my hand. He spoke to his wife, who stood, gently took the coffee pot from me, and went into the kitchen, looking quietly in the cabinets for cups.

I could still barely open my eyes. I sat at the breakfast table across from him. "Abdulhadi. Why are you here?"

"Oh, you don't remember? The computer, brother!" he took the large, old laptop out of the bag. "Yesterday morning - you said it had to be done at home." Noor sat down beside him.

"No, no. That's not —"

"You know," he said, wagging a finger in the air. "The believers in my country, we are so few. We depend on each other, just like this. It is the only way we have been able to survive. I am so blessed - *mabruk* - to find a believer like you so soon in this country. Praise be to the God and Father of our Lord Jesus Christ."

I stared at him and Noor, who now sat beside him.

"So," he said, "You know how to clean the virus?"

"Just give me the computer," I said.

"I thank God for you, *habibi*."

Questions

1. Because of his cultural differences, Abdulhadi unknowingly lacks a certain modesty ("shameless"). In what ways do you see this in his interactions with "Brother Yusuf?"

2. The "impudent" friend is commended in the parable, not as a model for our interactions with people, but with God. In what way are we allowed (or even commanded) to be "impudent" or "shameless" toward God?

3. On what basis is such an approach to God acceptable?

4. Abdulhadi doesn't take "no" for an answer (see the Parable of the Persistent Widow). How does that inform prayer life?

5. How is God similar to "Brother Yusuf?" How is he different?

Subversive Stories

THE PARABLE OF THE RICH FOOL
Luke 12:13-21

"Someone in the crowd said to [Jesus], "Teacher, tell my brother to divide the inheritance with me." But he said to him, "Man, who made me a judge or arbitrator over you?" And he said to them, "Take care, and be on your guard against all covetousness, for one's life does not consist in the abundance of his possessions." And he told them a parable, saying, "The land of a rich man produced plentifully, and he thought to himself, 'What shall I do, for I have nowhere to store my crops?' And he said, 'I will do this: I will tear down my barns and build larger ones, and there I will store all my grain and my goods. And I will say to my soul, "Soul, you have ample goods laid up for many years; relax, eat, drink, be merry."' But God said to him, 'Fool! This night your soul is required of you, and the things you have prepared, whose will they be?' So is the one who lays up treasure for himself and is not rich toward God."

A Dream Come True

"Oh, this view! I just can't get over this *view*!" Helen said as she slid open the curtains. She turned to her husband. "Darling, don't you just *love* this view?"

Henry came and stood beside her, coffee in hand. He took a deep breath through his nose and put his arm around her. They looked out the sliding doors at the ocean. "That is some view."

"It's been what, three years? Never gets old does it?"

"Never," Henry said.

They went out onto the porch, the warm sea breeze on their faces, and sat on the outdoor furniture. Henry did a sudoku. Helen sorted through the week's shell collection.

"Henry, look at this sundial shell. It's enchanting. Isn't it simply gorgeous?"

"That is quite a shell," he said. He pulled his phone from his pocket and looked at the stock market futures. He checked his 401k and let out a sigh. "Helen, did you know our investments are growing faster than we are spending them?"

"How fabulous! But I'm not surprised. You always were such

a *shrewd* investor."

"Do you realize we could live to be a thousand years old and, without working another day, be wealthier than we are now? Compound interest is a beautiful thing."

"Beautiful," Helen said, holding a shell up in the sunlight.

"Think of it - to be retired, at our age, in a place like this."

"Mm-hmm."

"And to not have to work another day. Don't have to lift a finger ever again." He laughed to himself. "Well, unless it's to swing a nine iron."

"You earned it, dear. You worked so hard and sacrificed so much for so many years. You deserve this - and more!"

"We both do." After a moment of silence, he said, "Hey, I've been thinking. . ." He stared out at sea.

She nudged him when he didn't continue. "And?"

"You know, I suppose we could just ride out our 401k for the rest of our lives, but we could also invest it in something that we could enjoy at the same time. You know, diversify our assets. Not have our eggs all in one basket."

"Isn't that why we got the mountain cabin?" she said.

"Right. But we still have 90% of our portfolio in stocks and bonds."

"Alright, well, do you want to buy another place?"

"No. Now, you might think I'm crazy, but . . ."

"Oh, quit teasing me! Out with it," she said.

"What if we got a yacht?"

Her eyes got big. She set her shells aside.

"What, you think I'm a fool?" he said.

"Oh, Henry, not at all. I think it's a *wonderful* idea! That's so much more fun than a boring old 401k."

"I'm so glad you're on board, pardon the pun."

"Of course. What else are we going to do with all that money? Like I said," she patted his hand, "Shrewd. Tell me where to sign." She thought for a moment. "You know Patty is *dying* of jealousy already," Helen said. "Just wait until she hears about the yacht. Fred's got another ten years before retirement."

"Poor guy. We should invite them out here sometime." He looked at the time on his watch. "Well, I'd better go walk the dogs. They'll be after me soon if I don't get going."

"Don't forget to give Chee Chee her arthritis pill. She likes it with a little peanut butter, you know," Helen said. "She gets so cranky without it, poor thing."

"I know, and she takes it out on Woopie." Henry slid open the door and two little dogs burst out, circling him and yapping.

"Told you they'd be after me!" he said, chuckling. "Alright, alright, you two, I'm coming." He went inside, changed, and laced up his favorite walking shoes.

"I'll be back!" he called toward the patio.

"Ok dear, I'm just going to rest my eyes for a bit. I think sorting through these shells has worn me out."

He went out the front door, down the stairs, and stepped onto the beachside walking path. The dogs stopped every fifty yards to sniff and investigate. The first stop, Henry looked through the piers and beams of the neighbor's house. The house was a timeshare, used by a dozen revolving families throughout the year. There were no cars in the driveway or carport, so he could see straight through the piers to the dune grass waving gently in the breeze on the near side of the beach. They had gotten to know a few of the timeshare families, even played a board game with one. He wondered which ones would come that summer. The house on the other side of them was owned by a New York couple who came down in the winter, who had proven impossible to get to know.

Fifty yards later, the dogs stopped again to sniff a mailbox. At the light ahead Henry saw a young family on the crosswalk, towing a wagon full of beach toys. The oldest child was pulling the wagon, the mother holding a toddler, the father holding the hand of another child. Henry tried to remember the beach trips he had taken his family on when they were that age, but he couldn't, which irritated him. *How can I not remember those trips?* He considered calling his son, Hank, when he got home, to see if he remembered their beach trips. He realized they hadn't spoken since Christmas, when Hank and his wife came with the grandkids. He began to feel bad. *No, I'm sure we've spoken since then.*

He continued on with the dogs. Woopie did his morning business on the neutral ground. Henry took a bag from his pocket, picked it up, and tied the bag, tossing it into the neighbor's trash. They walked for another ten minutes until he noticed Chee Chee, the Yorkie, limping. *Helen would kill me. I forgot her meds!* He decided to cut their morning walk short and turned around to head home.

He walked up the steps to his house, carrying Chee Chee under his arm. He was hoping to sneak the medicine to her when he got inside, but when he entered, he heard a strange sound.

"Helen?" he said. "Everything alright?" He put Chee Chee down on the floor. He traced the sound to one of the guest bedrooms, where he found Helen, sobbing and pacing the room.

"Helen! What's wrong?"

"Oh, Henry!" she came to him and put her arms around his neck. He felt the moisture of her tears through his shirt.

"Honey, what happened?"

"It's nothing. It's silly," she said, her head buried in his shirt. "You'll think I'm a fool."

"It must be *some*thing! Tell me."

"It's nothing really." She wiped her tears. "Just a dream." She took a deep breath. "I dozed on the patio for a few minutes while you were gone and had the most awful dream. Just *awful*."

"What happened?"

"No, really. It's not real. That's all that matters. You're here. That's all I need. Really. As long as you're here."

"Alright, then." He stroked her back. "Tell you what. I think I know what you need."

"Oh?"

"Yes, I've been thinking about doing this anyway. What would you think of going on a tiki boat cruise tonight?"

Helen laughed. "Oh, I haven't been on one in ages!"

"I know, I think it'll cheer you up. You need to relax, honey." He squeezed her shoulders. "We'll toast to the new yacht."

"I love it! We'll eat, drink, and be merry! That's why we're here, after all, isn't it?"

He looked at her, tilting his head. He blinked a few times. "What did you say?"

"I said I love it. Henry, why are you looking at me like that, dear?"

"What?" he said. "Oh, I was just going to say - Phil told me about the tiki cruises at the clubhouse last week. He and Sherry just went on one."

"It's a perfect idea, Henry." She kissed him on the cheek and began to leave the room. She paused and turned around slowly. "Just one thing."

"Sure."

"I don't have anything to wear for a tiki cruise." She bit her lip. "You think I could run down to that local place I like and grab one for the occasion?"

"Of course, you know you don't have to ask," he said. She kissed him again and walked away.

She called from the living room. "I wasn't going to go to Pilates, but I think I will now. Then I've got bridge at the clubhouse. After that I'll swing by and get the dress. And then we can head to the tiki place. Maybe 6:30?"

He stepped into the room. "Sure, we can catch the sunset."

"Such a lovely idea, Henry. You're a doll." She headed toward the door.

"Helen?"

She turned around, hand reaching for the door. "Yes, sweetie?" She stared at him, blinking and smiling.

"Never mind."

"That walk put you in a funny mood." She opened the door. "See you tonight!"

Henry stood in place, staring at the door for several minutes after she left. "Huh," he said finally. He walked to the sliding doors and looked out at the ocean. "It is quite a view, isn't it?"

He sat down at the breakfast table and ate a bowl of cereal, thinking about what he ought to do that day. "I have to pinch myself sometimes, Chee Chee, to make sure this life is real. Strange isn't it? Don't have to lift a single finger." He got up, poured himself some orange juice, and sat down again to his cereal. "Thirty-five years of corporate slavery. Now, a slave to no one," he said, looking down at the dog. "Except you of course!" He bent down and scratched her under her chin. "No one to tell me what to do, when or how to do it, where to go. No one," he said. "Nobody." He laughed. "Sometimes I kind of miss it. Isn't that funny?" He threw some cereal to the dog. "Woopie! Isn't that funny, old boy?"

He pushed his cereal bowl away when he finished. "I ought to call Hank." He got out his phone and called.

"Hey Dad."

"Hank! How are you kiddo?"

"I'm fine. How are you?"

"I was just telling Chee Chee about how I have to pinch myself sometimes to make sure life can really be this good. You know, like a dream?"

"Yeah, I get it. How's Mom?"

"Mom? Oh, well. The funniest thing. . ."

". . . Dad, you there?"

"Oh, hey!"

"What were you saying?"

"Huh? Oh, never mind. Hey, I was on a walk this morning and I thought of you. Has it been a while since we talked?"

"Since Christmas."

"How has it been that long? I can't believe how quickly time passes at my age. Sheesh, I'm sorry. Catch me up! How is everybody?"

"Well, you know about Beth and the miscarriage in February."

"Right! Oh, son. I am so sorry."

"It was really bad. The doctor said we shouldn't try for any more kids. Beth is crushed."

"Ah! I should have called. How did I not call?"

"Mom passed along your condolences."

"I know. I've got to do better though. You know, I've never been good at long-distance relationships. Out of sight, out of mind kind of thing. Well, besides that, y'all doing OK?"

"We're making it."

"Come on, that doesn't sound like the champion I know!"

"It is what it is. Working two jobs. Four kids, five and under. Not the easiest season." Hank paused. "You talk to Maggie lately?"

"Maggie?"

"Yeah, didn't Mom tell you? Tom broke it off."

"What! I had no clue. They seemed so in love."

"I know, it's totally crushed her. She's hardly left her apartment in months."

"Ah, more bad news! I better call her after you. I'll call her as soon as we're done. I'll make a note right now - Call Maggie."

"Hey, I'm on break. Was there something in particular you called for?"

"Oh, sure. It's nothing. Well, just one thing. I was walking the dogs this morning and . . . anyway, I was trying to remember our beach vacations when you and Maggie were young. No matter how hard I tried, I couldn't remember a thing about them."

"We went every year."

"I know! That's what I thought. Beach volleyball! Kites! Snorkeling! Sandcastles! How did I forget it all?"

Hank laughed. "No offense, Dad, but Mom was more of the beach parent. You always stayed inside on your computer."

"Oh?" Henry was taken aback. He began to feel bad again, but then added, "Well, I guess now I get to be the beach *grand*parent!"

"Well, hey, on that note: I don't think we're going to make it out there this summer. It's just too hard with the kids this young, especially for Beth. It'll be easier when they're older. Sorry. Can you break the news to Mom for me?"

"Aw, hey! We can help with the kids! You should come."

"Sorry, Dad. Maybe next summer."

"Ah! I get it. Maybe we'll come see *you* guys."

"Sure. Well, my boss is looking at me. I better go."

"Hang in there, bud."

Hank hung up. Henry stared at the blank screen of his phone. After a few minutes he stirred from his trance. "Now, what was I about to do?" He looked down at Chee Chee, who jumped into his lap. He scratched her behind her ears. "That's the thing, Chee Chee. Here in paradise, no one can tell me what to do, when or how to do it, where to go. No one," he said. "Nobody." Chee Chee gave a little Yorkie purr and licked his chin. "Oh! Good grief - your arthritis! I knew I was forgetting something." He got up and lost his balance for a moment. Catching himself on the kitchen bar, he waited until the dizziness went away. He went into the pantry and came back with a pill covered with peanut butter. "Sorry, I know the creamy is easier on your teeth, old girl, but we're out. I'll have to remember to get some at the Publix." He saw his phone on the breakfast table. "Oh, Maggie!" he said. He looked out at the ocean view and suddenly felt the urge to be productive. "No, I better get some things done first. I'll call first thing after lunch."

Henry went out on the patio. "Woopie!" he said. "Look at this perfect beach weather! Warm enough to go swimming but cool enough to take a nap in the shade. Maybe I'll go swimming. No - paddle boarding! That's what I'll do!" he said, looking out at the water. He yawned. "But first, I think I need a little catnap to clear my head. I can't believe how groggy I am this morning." He sat on the Adirondack chair and propped his feet up on the matching footstool. Within a few breaths, he was asleep.

"Henry? Henry, dear." Something was shaking him. "Henry!" someone shouted at him now, sounding alarmed.

"Huh?" he startled awake. "What's wrong?" He sat up. "What time is it?"

"Oh, Henry! I thought . . ." Helen let out a sigh. "It's five thirty, dear."

"Whew, I must've really needed some shuteye. Good grief, I slept for hours. I mean, all day." He wiped his mouth and laughed a little. "Drool! Am I that old?"

"It's Daylight Savings, I bet. You never do well with the time change."

"Huh."

"I got my dress," Helen said, standing up and pulling something out of a bag. "What do you think?"

"Dress?"

"For the tiki cruise!"

"Right!" He sat up straighter and rubbed his eyes. "Yeah, it's like one of those ... you know, the little dashboard dancers. What do you call them?"

"Hula girl?"

"That's it!"

"Isn't it perfect?"

"Hah, that is some dress! I'll go shower while you change." He stopped. "Ah! I forgot to call and make a reservation. Can you do it while I shower?"

"Of course, darling."

An hour later they stepped onto the tiki boat. Although there was room for fifteen to twenty people, they were the only people there besides the driver and bartender.

"Just the two of us, I guess! The whole boat to ourselves," Helen said. "How romantic." They went to the front and sat on a couple of bar stools at a small, high table. The bartender came to them. "Anything while you wait?"

"Mojito for me," Henry said.

"Excellent choice." He turned to Helen. "And for the lady? I love that dress by the way."

"Oh, you're sweet. A cosmo, please."

"I need to see some ID."

"Oh, stop it," she laughed. She took out her license. The bartender pretended to study it carefully and handed it back to her.

"I'll be back in a moment with your drinks and an *hors-d'oeuvres* list."

"Perfect," she said. She looked at Henry and giggled. "I wonder if we'll see dolphins tonight? Can you imagine? Dolphins on a sunset tiki cruise?"

They received their drinks and ordered a shrimp cocktail. The boat started and began moving out to sea. Helen looked at him, eyes sparkling, and raised her glass, "To the yacht!" she said. They clinked glasses. They both stared out to sea, neither of them speaking for several minutes. The waiter brought the appetizer.

"You know, Maggie used to love dolphins. Every summer she *begged* to dive with them."

"Oh, Maggie," Henry said to himself quietly. He felt bad and rubbed his temples. Several minutes went by. They sipped their drinks.

"Helen," Henry said, watching her swirl a shrimp in the cocktail sauce. "Do you ever wonder if . . ."

"What is it?" she said.

"Nah." He took a sip of his mojito and didn't say anything more.

"Please, what?" She sipped her cosmo.

"It's nothing."

"I know you! What is it? Is it the dress? It's too much isn't it?"

"No, it's not the dress."

"The yacht? You can't change your mind about the yacht, dear. I've already told everyone."

"No, no, it's not that either. I . . . I was talking to Hank today, after you left. He told me —"

"Oh, about the miscarriage? I know! Poor things. They've

been utterly *heart*broken."

"It's not just that, it's . . ." He looked down at his drink and said quietly, "Do you have any regrets?"

"Regrets? Where is *that* coming from?" She looked at him, but he didn't speak. "Well, sure. Everyone does."

"Tell me, Helen. What do you regret?"

"I don't know," she laughed. "What's gotten into you?" She sipped her drink.

"You didn't answer the question."

"Honey, I'm here to see dolphins! Not dwell on the past."

"Never mind the past. Do you regret . . ." he looked around, "This?"

"This cruise is delightful, dear." She sipped her drink and turned away from him, toward the sunset. The waiter came and she ordered another cosmo.

"No, Helen." He put his hand gently on her wrist.

"Oh, Henry, look! Dolphins!" She called to the boat driver. "Do you see the dolphins?" The driver smiled and nodded. She turned back to Henry, a wide smile on her face. "Ohh, it's like a dream!"

"Helen. Look at me."

She turned to him, a little irritated. "Have you forgotten why we came? 'Eat, drink, and be merry.' Isn't that why we're here? Isn't that the point?"

"Is it?"

She stared at him and sipped her drink. She tried to pull her arm away. "You're hurting me. For heaven's sake, can we wait—"

"My God, Helen! What's the point of it all?"

"Honey, you're slurring your words! I think you've had

enough to — oh, Henry, your face! What's wrong with your face?" Henry let go of her wrist and fell off the barstool to the deck of the boat.

"Henry? Oh God! Henry!" Helen dropped to her knees and held his head in her hands. "I'll answer the question now. You're just teasing, aren't you? You're teasing. Henry! Wake up you old fool!"

Questions

1. In what ways have Henry and Helen "laid up treasure for themselves" and neglected what matters most?

2. What false security do Henry and Helen have? Do you see anything similar in yourself?

3. Psalm 90:12 says, "Teach us to number our days that we may get a heart of wisdom." How does this relate to this parable and story?

4. How does Helen, in her own way, avoid the most important things in life? Why might she do so?

5. Henry "felt bad" several times in the story. What is going on in those moments? How does he respond?

6. Henry is struck several times about the "point" of life. What is the point of life? Does your life reflect your answer?

THE PARABLE OF THE DISHONEST MANAGER
Luke 16:1-9

"There was a rich man who had a manager, and charges were brought to him that this man was wasting his possessions. And he called him and said to him, 'What is this that I hear about you? Turn in the account of your management, for you can no longer be manager.' And the manager said to himself, 'What shall I do, since my master is taking the management away from me? I am not strong enough to dig, and I am ashamed to beg. I have decided what to do, so that when I am removed from management, people may receive me into their houses.' So, summoning his master's debtors one by one, he said to the first, 'How much do you owe my master?' He said, 'A hundred measures of oil.' He said to him, 'Take your bill, and sit down quickly and write fifty.' Then he said to another, 'And how much do you owe?' He said, 'A hundred measures of wheat.' He said to him, 'Take your bill, and write eighty.' The master commended the dishonest manager for his shrewdness. For the sons of this world are more shrewd in dealing with their own generation than the sons of light. And I tell you, make friends for yourselves by means of unrighteous wealth, so that when it fails they may receive you into the eternal dwellings."

Puddin' Head Harvey

"You're fired, Harvey."

Harvey sat back suddenly in his chair, mouth agape. "What? Me? Why?"

"You tell us." The seven elders stared at him, angry.

"How should I know? Has my preaching been too fiery? Have I been overzealous in care for my flock? What?"

"We know what you've been up to."

"I'm lost, guys. You tell me. This is truly a shock."

"Harvey, we had an audit done of the church's finances. Over the last five years you've embezzled almost five hundred thousand dollars."

"Me? Old Puddin' Head Harvey? I hardly know the PIN to my debit card, much less how to — what's the word you used — *embezzle* money." Harvey appeared surprised and hurt.

"Besides the cash, there's the ski boat and beach house."

"Now wait a second, those are used entirely for ministry purposes."

"A thirty-thousand dollar diamond necklace for your wife."

"Should I not love my bride as our Lord loves his church?"

"Four trips to Europe."

"Those were pilgrimages!"

"The African safari hunts —"

"Mission trips!"

"The Lamborghini."

"Wouldst thou muzzle the ox that treadeth out the corn?"

"I can't take it!" one of the elders stood up suddenly, his chair falling over. "The justification, the excuses. Get out! You're fired! It's not up for debate."

Harvey began to weep and beat his fist on the conference table. "You just throw out old Harvey, just like that? All because of a little misunderstanding about money? I built this church brick by brick. Does that mean nothing to you? Is money really worth tearing apart the kingdom?"

"Out!"

Harvey looked from elder to elder, studying for any sign of sympathy to his cause. He found none. Finally, he stopped crying and shrugged. "This is a mistake, fellas. The blood of an innocent man is on your hands, you hear? Anyway, I'll go. I'll go. Just give me two weeks. Two weeks to clean out my office. To say goodbye. These people are like children to me. Would you rob them of a chance to say goodbye to their father?"

"You've got until Friday."

He sighed. "Alright then. If it's like that."

"Goodbye, Harvey."

Harvey went home and began calling church members, but not to confess.

"I know, Mrs. Norris, I feel betrayed too. But such is the way of that old rugged cross. We can't expect a servant to be greater than his master."

"You're right, John, it *is* a conspiracy. A witch hunt. They're just looking for somewhere to pin the blame for the church's finances. I guess old Harvey can take the hit for the team."

"Yes ma'am, spiritual warfare is right. I just hate to see the Devil win like this. No doubt his craft and power are great."

"It reminds me of what the Good Book says, 'Through much tribulation do we enter the kingdom.' I suppose I don't mind it so much when I think of it that way."

"Armageddon? I didn't think of that, but now that you say it, you may be right. Yes, indeed, the great rebellion before the End."

Although not everyone was convinced, many believed him and became vehement defenders of Harvey. Word began to spread rapidly about the accusations and mistreatment he had received at the hands of the elders.

Next, Harvey began to give to various church members the many things he had purchased over the years with the church's money, both buying their favor and getting rid of evidence.

"My sweet wife said she couldn't bear to wear the necklace anymore, not after the accusations that have been leveled against her. You take it, take it and sell it and put the money towards world missions, brother."

"It's like the Lamborghini just showed up in my driveway one day, I tell you, fallen down from heaven like manna. Should I have despised the Lord's good gift? Apparently so. Anyway, it's yours now. What does a quiet old soul like me need with a toy like that?"

"The beach house and boat. Both of them, yes ma'am. The Lord just put it on my heart, that's all. I want to see them put to good use . . . A retreat center? In my name? Aw, you do what you want. As for me, my left hand knows not the work of my right."

By Friday, after sufficient slander and manipulation and prayer had taken place, his supporters were unanimous: it was time for Harvey to start his own church, a new one for the faithful remnant.

The first few times it was suggested, he seemed reluctant. "Oh, I don't know. I'm just feeling a little sore from it all, a little embarrassed by the accusations. I don't know if I'm up for another go. Maybe I'll just retire early."

His reluctance only increased the zeal of his supporters. Several people came by his home, imploring him to start a new church and not leave them behind to the wolves. "I have to say, friends, my compassion grows warm when you put it like that, like looking at sheep without a shepherd."

Finally, someone called and told him about an old church building for sale across the street from their current church. "We've got a donor who has agreed to buy the place, Harvey. The only condition the he gave was that you would agree to be its pastor."

"Well, Jehovah Jireh," he said. "Can a servant refuse his master or a child his father? Thy will be done, O Lord."

The elders were prepared to announce the news of Harvey's

embezzlement at the worship service on Sunday. After the guest preacher's sermon, they would inform the congregation and hold a Q&A, ending with a time of extended prayer. Yet, at the normal time of the service, the pews were only sparsely filled. Only a tenth of the congregation was in attendance. The elders went through with the service, confused and alarmed. Finally, just before the Q&A, a member took one of the elders by the arm and said, "I need to show you something." They led him out the church's front door. Across the street, a large hand-painted sign read, "Second Baptist Church, Reverend Harvey Humphrey." The doors of the newly established church were open wide, revealing a building filled with people. Families exited one by one, well-dressed and smiling. Just outside the door, shaking hands and receiving hugs from them all was Harvey.

"I'll be," the elder said slowly, taken aback. He walked across the street up to Harvey. The people around Harvey parted and stood by his side. "I'm going to be furious with you later. At the moment, though, I think I'm in shock. And, to be honest, I'm impressed. I don't know how you pulled this off."

"It's the Lord's doing, brother," Harvey said. "And it is marvelous in our eyes."

"No, no it's not his doing. It is certainly yours. You're a genius Harvey, however you've done it. A master of persuasion. Here's what I can't help but wonder. All these years, you've apparently had such gifts but never put them to good use. You've used them in secret to swindle the church rather than serve it. You use them now to manipulate a whole congregation into leaving and following after a crook like you. It's a shame, it really is, wasting your gifts on your own little kingdom."

"You know what that Old Book says, 'Wise as a serpent, innocent as a dove.'" Harvey winked at him. "Now, if you'll excuse me, old Puddin' Head Harvey's got a congregation to greet."

Questions

1. This parable can be perplexing. How would you summarize its main point?

2. What are Harvey's "gifts" and "skills?" How did he use them to swindle the church? How might he have used them to build up the church instead?

3. How does Matthew 10:16, which Harvey quotes at the end of the story, summarize the point of this parable?

4. Is there any way in which you are squandering the things God has given you on things that are sinful or unwise?

5. What are some examples of the kind of "shrewdness" Jesus is recommending to his followers?

The Parable of the Talents
Matthew 25:14-30

"For it will be like a man going on a journey, who called his servants and entrusted to them his property. To one he gave five talents, to another two, to another one, to each according to his ability. Then he went away. He who had received the five talents went at once and traded with them, and he made five talents more. So also he who had the two talents made two talents more. But he who had received the one talent went and dug in the ground and hid his master's money. Now after a long time the master of those servants came and settled accounts with them. And he who had received the five talents came forward, bringing five talents more, saying, 'Master, you delivered to me five talents; here, I have made five talents more.' His master said to him, 'Well done, good and faithful servant. You have been faithful over a little; I will set you over much. Enter into the joy of your master.' And he also who had the two talents came forward, saying, 'Master, you delivered to me two talents; here, I have made two talents more.' His master said to him, 'Well done, good and faithful servant. You have been faithful over a little; I will set you over much. Enter into the joy of your master.'

"He also who had received the one talent came forward, saying, 'Master, I knew you to be a hard man, reaping where you did not sow, and gathering where you scattered no seed, so I was afraid, and I went and hid your talent in the ground. Here, you have what is yours.' But his master answered him, 'You wicked and slothful servant! You knew that I reap where I have not sown and gather where I scattered no seed? Then you ought to have invested my money with the bankers, and at my coming I should have received what was my own with interest. So take the talent from him and give it to him who has the ten talents. For to everyone who has will more be given, and he will have an abundance. But from the one who has not, even what he has will be taken away. And cast the worthless servant into the outer darkness. In that place there will be weeping and gnashing of teeth.'"

A Patch of Ground

Tom, Matt, and Jud were in their last year of seminary. They'd spent three years studying for ministry. They had completed their academic courses in theology, church history, Greek, Hebrew, and hermeneutics, as well as their pastoral courses in preaching, counseling, discipleship and evangelism. They had been prepared in every way for their calling to ministry. Now it was time for their yearlong practicum, the capstone of the seminary's divinity program, where they would be placed in churches across the region as pastoral interns to apply their learning and test their skills. A handful of faculty and staff called the Ministry Practicum Committee was charged with overseeing the program.

Tom was beloved in seminary and yet the envy of all. In preaching class his trial sermon made his professor weep. His classmates were only half-joking about sensing the *shekinah* glory when he read and translated Hebrew. A bold defender of orthodoxy, he also stood up for the Korean students when he felt they weren't getting a fair shake in class. He organized panel discussions and prayer meetings, gathering both professors and students alike. Tom's effortless success would have made him intolerable to the lower achieving students if he weren't utterly unaware of himself. You couldn't help but want to follow him.

When it came time for Tom's practicum, the seminary connected him with a historic downtown church in need of an interim pastor. The church had incredible potential to grow, given its history, location, and facilities. At the same time, it was full of challenges. It had lost its pastor due to a church split, which had left it full of residual hard feelings and pessimism. Being downtown, just to get through the doors of the church required dealing with homeless panhandlers, drug pushers, and the mentally ill, keeping half the members from even attending worship. Lastly, the church's membership was aging, making it increasingly difficult to appeal to the younger generation. The seminary told the church's pastoral search committee they believed he would be "catalytic" for the church, even as an interim pastor. The church, due to its recent disappointment in leadership, was dubious, but agreed to try him out.

Matt was not omni-gifted like Tom, but after his second year in seminary he felt like he found both his place among the student body and his calling. To Matt, preaching felt constrictive and unbearably formal, leaving him with little appetite for it. He made passing grades in the more academic courses but found them depressingly boring and cold. Ordinary in most areas, Matt's passions and giftings converged remarkably in his relational abilities. When you sat down with Matt, even for the first time, it felt like speaking with an old friend to whom you wanted to bear your soul. His classmates often asked to study with him because, they said, his personal approach helped them "feel" the truth. At the same time, what he had in emotional depth and spiritual maturity did not help him in more public leadership, where he was fairly ineffective.

The seminary found Matt an unpaid internship in a large church of several thousand members, who expressed a need for personal discipleship among its members. The Committee felt that the opportunity would be suitable to him, because he would primarily be practicing a "private ministry of the Word," rather than public. There would be some challenges for him, though. The church was a well-oiled machine, excelling in its organizational structure, programs, and operations. At the same time, it had perhaps succeeded too much in this area, and many members complained that it no longer felt like a family as it had in its earlier days. "We've become all trellis and no vine," the senior pastor told Matt. The charge given to Matt was to find a way to cultivate more organic relationships and ministry within the church. The Ministry Practicum Committee thought Matt could do it, having seen his gifts at work, but the church leadership wasn't so sure he'd be able to swim upstream enough to make a difference.

And then there was Jud, whom no one really knew much about. He didn't speak much in class, and when he did it wasn't memorable. In fact, if any of his fellow seminarians had passed him in the grocery store or seen him at a restaurant, although they would have recognized him, they would not have been able to place where they knew him from. This was not because Jud was ignored or intentionally left out. He simply lived in the shadows. Afraid of his ego being bruised, he never tried hard on his papers, for how would that reflect on his intelligence if he actually tried and *then* failed? Thus, he always turned in shoddy work. He hid from the Dean of Chapel, terribly afraid that he might be asked to speak at one of the student chapels. When it came time for the seminary to match him with a church, the Ministry Practicum Committee said, "Now, who is Jud again?" They didn't know what to do with him, having never seen him apply himself.

After much searching and scratching of the head, the seminary found Jud a gig as a part-time youth director at a small rural church. The handful of youth who attended were ordinarily led by a retired schoolteacher, whose ministry had not been remarkable, but he had at least gathered them together consistently, taught them the Bible, and took interest in their individual lives. The youth were not the brightest group, but they were teachable; not the most eager participants, but they showed up. The church's ambitions for the group were not grand: "All we're looking for is a leader young enough to connect to these kids." The seminary, not knowing anything about Jud, at least knew that he was young, and felt that the assignment would be easy enough.

Tom's success at the historic downtown church surprised everyone, including Tom himself. Always an avid student of church history, he delved into the records and stories of the church's past, which went back two hundred years. He began to share what he was learning with the session of elders, who were so intrigued they encouraged him to share his research with the church. He had a series of luncheons after the worship service, where he did just that. The historical perspective helped the membership begin to look past the recent church split and pastoral failure and gave them a sense of corporate identity and rootedness. Tom asked the practicum committee for their wisdom about the less savory characters who loitered outside the church doors. As a result of committee's advice, he got the media team to set up a speaker outside the door to broadcast the service into the street. The effect was marvelous. Many of those who loitered outside the door heard the gospel and believed and joined the church; the rest simply got tired of hearing it and found somewhere else to go. Tom gathered a handful of people and helped them start an AA group. Unintentionally, this change in the demographic of the membership gave the church an "edgy" vibe, attracting a younger crowd. Thus, in less than a year of interim pastoral work, Tom had gotten the church out of its rut and into a new season of flourishing.

At the end of the year, when his time at the church was coming to a close, the Ministry Practicum Committee sat down with him. "Tom, we've talked it over with the church and their search committee. They've been so pleased with what has taken place over the last year, they want to extend you the position of Senior Pastor permanently. Well done! We gave you a patch of ground to work and keep, and you have served it faithfully. May you enjoy a long and fruitful ministry."

Matt's success was not as effortless as Tom's. He did, indeed, have to swim upstream at the large church. For the first six months his ideas and methods were resisted by the very leaders who appointed him. He preached several times but was not received very well. He was useless in staff meetings and a mess administratively. Most in his position would have given up or given in to the prevailing philosophy of ministry, but Matt simply knew no other way of doing things. "It's just going to take time," he kept telling them. His only initial request was for a meal stipend, which he used almost daily to take members to coffee and lunch and to have leaders and their families over for dinner. The church's leadership team was unsure, saying, "The results just aren't very measurable." The first half of the practicum, Matt often had to lean on the seminary committee for encouragement. If it weren't for them, he would not have been able to persevere to the end.

Finally, after the first six months, things began to change. Members began to come to him for counseling, feeling personally connected to a pastor for the first time in many years. The word spread, and the work began to grow. He gathered a handful of like-minded, relational lay leaders in the church and asked if they'd help with some of the counseling and discipleship. The pastoral staff slowly began to change their minds about him. Eventually they asked what he thought of using the empty building space to create an official counseling center. "I'll do it if you think that's best," he said, "but maybe we should let the vine grow a bit on the trellis that's already there." The team was impressed with his answer and let him continue in his own way. By the end of his practicum year, although there were no numbers they could report nor programs they could add to the website, Matt's swim upstream had undoubtedly begun to change the culture of the church and, even more impressive, added a new, personal flavor to the staff's philosophy of ministry.

At the end of the year, when his ministry practicum was coming to a close, the committee sat down with him. "Matt, we've talked it over with the church and their pastoral staff. Although they can't put their finger on how exactly you've done it, they've been so pleased with what has taken place over the last year, they have offered you the position of Associate Pastor of Discipleship. Well done! We gave you a patch of ground to work and keep, and you have served it faithfully. May you enjoy a long and fruitful ministry."

When Jud heard of his classmates' internship assignments to different churches and ministries, he considered dropping out of seminary altogether. He could not imagine being in a situation like Tom, with the odds stacked against him, or having to swim upstream like Matt. Yet when he finally received his assignment, it was not with anxiety but with a sense of wounded pride. "Really? This is all they think I'm good for?" he asked himself when he walked out of the meeting.

The first youth group gathering he led at the rural church, only four students showed up. The next two meetings, only six. When he asked why nobody was coming, the pastor said, "Four, six students? That ain't nobody. Care for what you've got and see if the Lord don't bless it." Unfortunately, just like in his coursework, Jud was afraid to apply himself to the work. He prepared last minute for his teachings and canceled close to half the weekly gatherings. It took months before he could remember the names of the kids. Most of his time at the church was spent critiquing the pastor and feeling like he was worthy of a better assignment. On the other hand, he thought of Tom and Matt often, pitying himself for his lack of gifts and meager opportunities. By the end of the year's practicum, the students loathed him, several swearing not to return until he was gone.

Finally, when his internship with the youth was coming to a close, the seminary committee sat down with him. "Jud, we've been talking with the church and its pastor. It doesn't sound like you really applied yourself. What happened?"

"I guess I'm just not as gifted as some of these other guys," he said. "I'm not the all-star you want me to be."

"But Jud, that's no excuse. No one was asking you to be an all-star."

"I knew what y'all expected of me. Some big success story, right? A revival! I could never have achieved what someone like Tom has. I'm no miracle worker. I'm no Billy Graham."

"You didn't even try. You're wrong, we never expected those kinds of things from you. All we wanted you to do was make the best of the opportunity you had and to apply your training and education. We never heard from you once. In fact, we reached out to you a dozen times to see if we could help, but you didn't respond."

"If I would have been honest you'd have hammered me."

"Jud, we gave you a patch of ground to work and keep, and

you squandered it. And that youth group is far worse off now because you were too full of pride and self-pity to accept your lot, and too fearful to apply yourself to it.

"You guys set me up for failure," Jud said.

"I'm sorry to do this, we have no choice but to fail you. Your shot at ministry is done, we can't in good conscience recommend you for ordination."

Jud rushed out of the meeting before anyone could see him cry. He headed home to seek his wife's sympathy and to look for a secular job.

Questions

1. In what ways did Jud bury his talent in the ground? What does it mean to "bury a talent?"

2. Why does Jud not apply himself in seminary or in his practicum?

3. What does Jud fundamentally misunderstand about the committee's expectations? How does this reflect the "one-talent" servant's misunderstanding of his master?

4. What "patch of ground" has been given to you? Think both in spiritual and earthly terms. What does it mean to faithfully "work and keep" that patch of ground?

5. Is there any gift or resource that God has given you to steward that you have buried instead?

Subversive Stories

THE PARABLE OF THE UNFORGIVING SERVANT
Matthew 18:21-35

"Then Peter came up and said to him, "Lord, how often will my brother sin against me, and I forgive him? As many as seven times?" Jesus said to him, "I do not say to you seven times, but seventy-seven times.

"Therefore the kingdom of heaven may be compared to a king who wished to settle accounts with his servants. When he began to settle, one was brought to him who owed him ten thousand talents. And since he could not pay, his master ordered him to be sold, with his wife and children and all that he had, and payment to be made. So the servant fell on his knees, imploring him, 'Have patience with me, and I will pay you everything.' And out of pity for him, the master of that servant released him and forgave him the debt. But when that same servant went out, he found one of his fellow servants who owed him a hundred denarii, and seizing him, he began to choke him, saying, 'Pay what you owe.' So his fellow servant fell down and pleaded with him, 'Have patience with me, and I will pay you.' He refused and went and put him in prison until he should pay the debt. When his fellow servants saw what had taken place, they were greatly distressed, and they went and reported to their master all that had taken place. Then his master summoned him and said to him, 'You wicked servant! I forgave you all that debt because you pleaded with me. And should not you have had mercy on your fellow servant, as I had mercy on you?' And in anger his master delivered him to the jailers, until he should pay all his debt. So also my heavenly Father will do to every one of you, if you do not forgive your brother from your heart."

Before and After

BEFORE AND AFTER. How could last Friday not be the dividing line between Sean's life as it once was and as it is now? The event of last Friday was so historic and life-altering, everything else could not help but be defined by it. Now three days into the After, Sean's mind was busy re-indexing his old memories, especially those involving his wife, putting them in the Before folder, where they could be grieved and, hopefully, forgotten.

It was Monday, and Sean had been at the grocery store for two hours, though he'd had such a hard time concentrating, his basket held no more than a handful of items. He was now in the freezer aisle, staring at a box of corn dogs, trying to understand the sale being offered. *It says 2 for $10. Do I have to buy two boxes to get the deal? Or does it apply to just one?* He couldn't figure it out. Occasionally someone would pass by and look at him. *If only they knew!* He promised himself that he would never again take for granted that the people he saw in public were not in pain. When an employee came and began stocking the freezer next to him, Sean wanted to tell him what had happened, to ask if he knew what it was like. At the same time, if the employee had wrapped his hands around Sean's neck and begun to squeeze, he would not have fought back. He would not have minded.

Finally, the worker turned to him. "Can I help you with something, sir?"

"It says 2 for $10," Sean said, his voice quavering. His eyes began to tear up. "Do I have to buy two boxes to get the deal? Or can I just buy one?"

"Oh, I'm sorry. The discount applies to one as well. They're just trying to get you to buy more, sorry for the confusion . . . is there something else?"

Sean stared at him blankly. "No. I guess I'll just get two. Thanks." Sean dumped the boxes in his grocery basket and pushed it to the dairy aisle.

He reached for a quart of caramel macchiato creamer but stopped, dropping his hand to his side after a moment. *No, that was Before.* He got a pint of half & half and kept moving. When he finally arrived at the register, he realized he forgot the eggs. On his way, he passed the wine section, his eye catching a fine merlot on sale that Samantha used to order at restaurants. He read the label on the back, then he read it again. His third time through he stopped, set it down and got a 12 pack of cheap beer. *This is After.*

When he got back to the register to check out, Sean looked up and saw his neighbor Brent walking his way. Part of him was desperate for Brent to come and talk to him and ask how he was doing. Another part of him hoped Brent didn't see him. Sean thought of leaving his basket and running to his car. Split between the two, he froze.

Brent saw him and walked quickly to him. "Sean!" he said, embracing him. "Ah, man, I can't believe it. Julie told me. I can't believe it. I've been trying to reach you. I came by the house. You OK? No, of course not. Ah, I wish I knew what to say."

"Me too," Sean said.

"Were you totally blindsided?"

"Completely."

"I think we all were. I know Julie and I were. How long's it been going on? Do you know?"

"I don't know. Probably a while."

"You heard from her since Friday?"

Sean looked at the floor and finally choked out, "No."

The cashier was looking at them. "Here," Brent said, "Let me help you." Brent loaded his groceries on the checkout conveyor belt while Sean leaned on the shelves of candy and wept. Brent paid for his groceries and put his arm around Sean and said, "Come on, let's get to the car. I'll meet you at your house."

The first week of the After, Sean spent hours at a time lying in bed, watching the ceiling fan slowly turn. *I've been trying to get back in shape. How could I let myself go like this?* He'd stare at the shelves in the living room, select a book and thumb through it mindlessly, and then toss it onto the coffee table, where there was now a pile of books. *She wanted to go to Europe, but I said no. Why do I have to be such a tightwad?* He'd walk to the kitchen and look in the refrigerator, though without an appetite. *I got her lingerie for our anniversary. Was that selfish? Why didn't I get her jewelry?* He'd lay on the couch with the TV on, without a clue what he was watching. *I used to leave her notes saying I was thankful for her, that I loved her. I'm so blind, how did I not notice the spark had gone out?* At the end of the day, he had no recollection of how he had spent his time because his mind was turned desperately inward, trying to understand what he had done wrong. After rummaging through the past for answers, he would always end up back at the same question, which was the most painful of all for its clarity. *Why doesn't my wife love me?*

After a week of such inner dialogue and conversations with his parents and with Brent, Sean was able to say, though without much conviction, 'It's not my fault.' Sure, he had things to own, he had things he should have done differently. He had regrets. At the same time, now he could at least tell himself that her infidelity was her own choice and not caused by him.

Even so, it was a battle. It was easier to be angry with himself. It was much harder to be angry at Samantha, whom he still loved. Every time he would come to believe it truly was not his fault, his mind would immediately begin to look for somewhere to place the blame for the wounds he carried. He would burn in anger towards Samantha for a moment, and then recoil. *No. I don't want to hate her. There must be another way.*

That Friday was on replay in his mind and he couldn't make it stop. He remembered exactly where he was on his commute to work. He had just dropped the kids off at school and was at the red light just before the on-ramp to the interstate when Julie called. She was breathless on the phone. "Sean, you need to get home. Now. I think Samantha's having an affair."

He remembered the metallic taste in his mouth when he saw the strange car in the driveway, the smell of a cologne not his when he entered the house and ascended the steps to the bedroom. Everything after that was a blur. He hoped it stayed that way. The last thing Sean remembered from that morning was Samantha's last words to him. "He's everything to me. I've made my choice." She ran out of the house and got into the strange car and drove away.

Sean was not angry for more than a moment at a time until his children came back from his parents' house, at the end of his week of mindless grief.

"Will Mommy be home for dinner?"

"Is Momma picking us up from school today or you?"

"Can you tell Mommy to come tuck me in?"

When Sean thought of the flash flood of pain that was about to swallow up his children, he finally accepted that he was not to blame for this. It was Samantha who had brought this curse down upon his children. His anger towards her peaked at the end of the third week, when he decided he had to give them some explanation. While they were at school, the third Friday since *that* Friday, he burned in anticipation of the moment, that afternoon, when he would have to feed poison to his children, telling them that their mother had abandoned them. They too, he realized, would have a Before and an After.

But things changed suddenly when he heard a car door slam outside. He was in his bedroom upstairs. The door chime sounded. Sean began to descend the stairs to see who it was. When he turned on the landing, he saw Samantha at the bottom of the stairs.

"I'm so sorry, Sean. I made a terrible mistake." She shrugged her shoulders. "I don't know what I was thinking."

Sean walked down the steps, past her, and into the living room. "Let's sit," he said, trying his best to keep his anger under control. They sat on opposite ends of the couch.

"How long?" Sean said quietly. "How long have you been seeing him?"

"Just that once."

"Samantha," he said. "Either tell me the truth or leave."

"OK, I know," she said, looking down. "I'm afraid to tell you."

"The truth or leave."

She took a deep breath. "Next month would be five years."

Sean felt concussed. He closed his eyes and thought for a while. "Why are you here?"

Samantha got up suddenly and fell at his feet and leaned her head into his lap. "I realized what I had thrown away for him. When I thought of you and the children, I just decided I couldn't go through with it. He wasn't worth it." She began to sob. "Oh, Sean! What have I done!"

"You've destroyed our family. Our marriage."

"I know! I know! But we can get through this!"

"How? What option do I have besides divorce? And it's not even my choice. You chose it when you decided to leave. You chose it for the last five years. What other choice do we have? The marriage is dead." He shook his head. "I've had a corpse for a marriage the last five years and didn't even know it."

Her mascara mingled with the tears that ran down her cheeks, leaving black streaks on her face. "No! No, we can make it through this. I love you, Sean. And I don't want the kids to go through a divorce. We'll get a marriage counselor. I'll find a therapist. I'll do the work, I swear." She looked up and saw that he wasn't convinced. "Oh, Sean! You deserve a faithful wife. You do! A loyal wife." She cried. "Give me another chance! I can be the wife you deserve."

Sean closed his eyes again and breathed. "Is it over?" he said. "Did you end it?"

"It's over!" she said in a shrill voice. "I swear! It's over. I blocked him on everything. I told him I'd call the cops if he ever showed up at the house or at work. It's done!"

Sean looked at the family portrait above the fireplace, a picture from Before if there ever was one. He no longer felt any grief. The idea of blaming himself now felt ridiculous. Instead, he was considering how to hurt her the way she'd hurt him. He was feeling for the softest spot in her conscience to insert his sharpest words.

"Please," she said, grabbing his hands. "Please, I have no one. Sean, please, don't do this." Her body was shaking. Her hair was in her face and had mixed with her makeup and tears. She looked wretched. She looked as wretched as he felt. She hardly looked human.

He felt the anger go out of him and then, only weariness. "I forgive you."

She wept a long time on his lap, thanking him over and over. Eventually, she sat up and wiped her face and pushed her hair back, putting it in a neat bun. They made small talk about the kids, about dinner, about work. "Well, I'm going to go wash my face and then pick up the kids from school." She began to walk away and then turned back. "Hey, just one question. How'd you know?"

"Huh?"

"How'd you figure it out? Just curious."

"Julie told me," he said.

Samantha narrowed her eyes. "Oh, right. Julie," she said. After a moment in the bathroom she went outside.

Sean went upstairs to the bedroom to lay on the bed and think. Before long he heard a raised voice outside. Pushing the curtains aside, he looked out the window and saw Samantha parked in front of Brent and Julie's house, red-faced, shouting out of the car window and honking her horn. Sean opened the window to hear what she was saying.

"I know you hear me! Come on out, you little rat. Come out and face me!" Samantha laid on the horn.

Julie stepped outside onto her porch.

"You," Samantha said in a low growl. "Of all people, you!"

"What?"

"Don't play games with me, you little squeaker. You just couldn't keep it in, huh? The gossip was too good not to share. You couldn't help but squeak, you little rat."

"Samantha, how could I not?"

"Great question - how could you not? Little pig that you are, how could you not squeal? I'll tell you how. It's called loyalty, Julie. Faithfulness. Does our friendship mean nothing to you?"

"Samantha, please. Come inside. Let's talk, ple—"

"No, of course it doesn't," Samantha screamed, "You had no right - *no right* - to stick your fat pig nose in my business." Suddenly Samantha's voice got low and quiet. Sean leaned out the bedroom window to hear better. "Get ready, Julie. All the dirt I've got on you? Girl, give me 24 hours, see what happens to your happy little life."

"Samantha, what? Please, try to understand. What was I supposed to do?"

"Lawyer up. That's all I'm saying. 'Cause I've got dirt on you, boo. And it'll be in the headlines tomorrow." Samantha rolled up her window and sped down the street. Julie ran into her house crying.

Sean opened the French doors to the balcony and watched Samantha turn at the corner and disappear. "I really had forgiven you," he said. "But now I see what it meant to you."

He looked out at the yard and didn't feel weary any longer. He turned into the bedroom and noticed all her things. Things from Before. He took her jewelry box from the table in the corner and launched it into the front yard. It exploded when it hit the ground, jewelry flying into the yard. Sean felt lighter. He went into the closet and removed her dresses and threw them off the balcony, watching them float down into the bushes below. Each item that went over seemed to ease something within him. He took the drawers out of the armoire and dumped them overboard, heaping underwear, yoga pants, and lingerie on top of the dresses. He took the sheets off the bed and threw them out. He looked at the pile for a while, feeling like there was something else, one more thing to complete the removal of his wife from the intimacy of his bedroom. He looked around for anything that was not theirs but hers. Finally, he went to the dark, oak vanity next to the closet, dragged it onto the balcony, and hoisted it over the railing. It fell to the ground, the mirror shattering and wood splintering.

Sean looked at the mess in the yard for a while. At first, he felt relieved and said, "So this is the After. Easier for me this way, I guess." A few minutes passed, and his anger cooled. Still relieved, a new grief overcame him, no longer for himself or his children, but for Samantha. "It didn't have to be this way. Why couldn't you have just let it go with Julie?" he said aloud. He replayed in his mind the conversation he'd just overheard. "I think I know why," he said. He turned and went back into the bedroom to call his attorney.

Questions

1. Forgiveness is costly. How do you see this in Sean? How do you see this in Christ?

2. What does Sean see in Samantha that causes him to "pity" her and forgive? Similarly, what does God see in us?

3. How does Samantha "choke" Julie? Why does this cause Sean to change his mind about forgiving her? What does it reveal about her "repentance?"

4. What warning does this story / parable give to someone who refuses to forgive?

5. What wisdom does this story / parable provide to someone who knows they need to forgive, but are struggling to do so?

PART 3
PARABLES OF THE KINGDOM

THE PARABLE OF THE HIDDEN TREASURE
Matthew 13:44

"The kingdom of heaven is like treasure hidden in a field, which a man found and covered up. Then in his joy he goes and sells all that he has and buys that field."

See also: *The Parable of the Pearl of Great Price*

The Commerce Comet

"Wʜᴀᴛ's ɪɴ ᴛʜᴇ ʟᴏᴄᴋʙᴏx?" I asked.

"Huh?" Jimmy sat on his bean bag chair, shoveling chips in his mouth.

"The lockbox." I pointed. "Up there at the top of your closet."

Jimmy glanced up briefly from the TV. "Oh, just some old baseball cards."

"Anything good in there?"

"I don't know. I haven't looked at them in years. You know I'm not a sports guy."

I couldn't quit staring up at the lockbox. A few minutes passed. Jimmy laughed at something on the TV. "Can I take a look at them?" I asked.

"They used to be the General's. Why do you care so much?" he said, an edge coming into his voice. Jimmy's dad was a high-ranking general in the Air Force who treated the home like a military barracks during his visits. Jimmy played the part of an orderly soldier when he was there, but the rest of the year he lived like an animal.

"Just curious," I said, "I used to collect them."

He finally turned toward me. "Listen. When he gave it to me a few Christmases ago, I thought it was some kind of treasure, being in a lockbox like that." Jimmy put the bag of chips down, reached over, and put a hand on my shoulder. He began to impersonate his father's deep, sanctimonious voice, lifting his chin and looking off into the distance. "'James, son, inside of this safety box you'll find the tokens of a great American tradition. My father passed them down to me, now I pass them on to you. True patriots that inspired me to become the man that I am. May they do the same for you.' I'd no clue what he was talking about. I opened up the box all excited to see what was inside and couldn't believe it - a bunch of junky old cards. Most of those guys are too old to even swing a bat, if they're even alive still. Who regifts a Christmas present to their kid? I felt like he wanted me to salute him or something. I just told him, 'Thank you, sir,' came straight to my room and shoved the box up in the closet, where it's sat ever since."

My hands began to sweat when I heard him say the cards were old. My cousin had taught me a lot about baseball cards and had given me some of his collection when he went off to college. "So, can I take a look at 'em?"

He turned back to the TV screen and waved his hand as if to say, "Go for it."

I brought a chair to the closet, stood on it and carefully took the lockbox down from the shelf. The key was still in it. I turned it and opened the lid.

The cards were in complete disarray but not in bad shape.

Hundreds, maybe a couple of thousand cards. None were in cases or sleeves. For the most part, I found the collection to be unremarkable. A Cal Ripken from the mid-eighties. An early Tony Gwynn. The oldest I recognized was a Nolan Ryan from the mid-seventies. Although my knowledge of baseball before the seventies was limited, I at least knew the hall of famers. I didn't see any, so I looked at some of the stats on the back of the cards. Again, nothing remarkable. I laid the cards out carefully on the carpet as I sorted through them.

"Like I said, a bunch of junk, huh?" Jimmy called over his shoulder, snorting.

"They're OK," I said, continuing to shuffle through. I had just about looked through them all when I saw it.

No.

Can't be.

Yes.

Holy smokes.

No.

Yes, it really is.

I had to read the card five times front and back to believe it, to make sure it wasn't some kind of reprint. The Commerce Comet. The Mick. Muscles. *For crying out loud, it's Mickey Mantle.*

"Anything good?" Jimmy asked.

"I dunno," I said quickly, short of breath. "Maybe."

And not just any Mickey Mantle. A 1952 Topps Mickey Mantle rookie card. And as far as I could tell, it was still in mint condition. My hands were so sweaty and shaky I was afraid I'd damage it. I put it at the bottom of the lockbox and buried it with the rest of the cards.

"Hey, Jimmy," I tried to sound nonchalant. "How much you want for these?"

He turned around at the mention of money.

"Oh, I don't know. The General probably wouldn't want me to sell it." Jimmy was playing hard ball.

"Twenty dollars?" I asked casually.

He looked at me suspiciously. Thrusting a few more chips in his mouth, he leaned forward and took the lockbox from me. He looked through some of the cards on top, his greasy fingers fouling up each one he touched. "I'll sell 'em, but if I'm going to risk the trouble of the General finding out, you've gotta make it interesting."

"Fifty dollars?" I said.

He kept sorting through the cards, devaluing them one by one with his oily touch. Head still down, he looked at me out of the corner of his eye and said, "Keep going." He was enjoying this.

I got desperate, anxious to seal the deal before he got to Mickey with his potato chip hands. "I'll give you my Xbox!"

That one surprised him. He knew how much I loved my Xbox, but I knew how jealous he was of it. He sat back and shifted his bulk around in his bean bag chair. Although Jimmy's mom was a bit of a pushover and did a lot for him that the General didn't know about, she had not yet given into his pleas for a game console.

Knowing I had him, I quickly added a condition to the sale. "But if your dad ever asks where the cards are you can't tell him you sold it to me."

"Deal." He slid the lockbox toward me across the carpet and

laughed. "He's way too worried about national security to have time to keep tabs on the junk in my closet. And trust me, I don't want him knowing I sold them either. I'll tell him we gave it to Goodwill. Hey, where you going?"

"I'll be right back," I said, taking the lockbox and heading outside.

I walked as quickly as I dared down the street to my house and gently put the lockbox under my bed. I ripped my Xbox out of the wall, threw it in a suitcase with its games and controllers, and, without pausing for a breath, ran back and tossed the bag on Jimmy's bed. He laughed. "Geez, you're such a chump. I would have just given them to you if you hadn't made such a big deal about it. Oh, and if my mom asks, I'm just going to tell her you got tired of video games and gave it away," he said.

"Perfect," I said, heading back out the door.

"Hey, come back. Let's hook it up and play."

"Sorry, I've got something better to do."

I left Jimmy's house but hardly got down his driveway before erupting in laughter. I lost my balance and fell, scraping my palms and knees on the concrete. I turned over and lay there for a moment, staring up at the sky, a little dazed. I looked at my chafed palms and noticed blood running down my legs. I would have groaned had I not remembered. Once again the volcanic joy came forth from deep inside, and I laughed like an idiot, lying on the driveway. I got to my feet and leapt and hollered all the way home, like a Yankee at the end of game seven of the 1962 World Series. A car drove by slowly, the driver rubbernecking. Someone peeked through their blinds, wondering about the commotion. I didn't care. I had something worth more than all the houses and cars on the block put together. Having said that, when I got home and entered my room, I couldn't help but notice, a little wistfully, the empty spot beneath the TV where my Xbox used to be.

I reached under my bed and went through the lockbox until I found the One. Using one of my old cases, I tossed aside the card that was in it and carefully put Mickey inside, screwing it tight. I studied the front and back of the card for a good half hour. I couldn't quit smiling and shaking my head. Finally, I put Mickey and the rest of my collection in the lockbox, which I placed in the blank spot under the TV. I locked it, put the key in a hiding place, and laid in bed, reveling as I stared up at the ceiling. I closed my eyes, satisfied.

My mom came into the room and gasped. "Honey, what happened to your legs?"

"What do you mean?" I said, my eyes still closed.

"And where's your Xbox?" she asked.

"What Xbox?"

She sighed. "What's gotten into you?"

I smiled.

Questions

1. In what way does the boy narrating "sell all he has" for the cards? Is that difficult for him? Why not?

2. The man in the parable (and the boy) is happy to give up everything he has ("in his joy") to gain the treasure in the field. How does that speak to the life of the Christian and the sacrifices we are called to make?

3. The boy falls and hurts himself on the way home but doesn't seem to mind. Why not? How does this speak to the cross-bearing and suffering a believer undergoes for the sake of Christ?

4. Describe the boy's joy on his way home. Does he regret his decision? How can you tell?

5. What "treasure" is gained by following Christ? What is sold in order to gain that treasure?

The Parable of the Mustard Seed
Matthew 13:31-32

"The kingdom of heaven is like a mustard seed, which a man took and planted in his field. Though it is the smallest of all seeds, yet when it grows, it is the largest of garden plants and becomes a tree, so that the birds come and perch in its branches."

See also: *The Parable of the Leaven*

A Pandemic

"Momma, what's COVID?" Ruthie asked as her mother tucked her into bed.

"Why do you ask that?" her mother said.

"I heard my teacher say it today."

"Oh, well, it's a type of virus. Kind of like a cold or the flu." Her mother turned on the night light and kissed her on the forehead. "All right, good night, honey."

Just as her mother was stepping out of the room, Ruthie said, "What's so special about it?"

Her mother stopped in the hallway and came back into the room. "What do you mean?"

"Well, my teacher said COVID once ruled the world."

"I guess that's one way to put it."

"Well," Ruthie said, a little impatient, "What's so special about it? Tell me the story. How did a virus rule the world?"

Her mother paused and looked at her watch. She looked at Ruthie, eyes wide and eager, and sat down on the bed.

Her mother took a deep breath. "Now, before I tell you

about it, just know that not everyone agrees about COVID. How it got started, where, why, and who. I'll just tell you one theory - one story - I've heard."

"K," Ruthie said, pulling the covers up to her chin.

"One thing we do know for sure - keep this one thing in mind while I tell the story - one thing that made COVID so special is that it was *very* contagious, more than normal viruses. Do you know what that means?"

"Yes, Momma. Tell me the story."

"All right. Years ago, before you were born, there was a bat."

"A bat?"

"Yes. A very small bat. Maybe the size of my thumb." Her mother held up her thumb.

"Aw, it's so cute!"

"Yes, and that cute little bat lived in a place called China, a country on the other side of the world."

"That place that makes all my toys."

"Yes. That place. And that bat carried a microscopic - that means teeny tiny - virus on its fur, as many bats do. Well, one night that bat left the cave where it lived."

"Why would it leave home?"

"Who knows? Maybe it was just looking for food. So, the little bitty bat left its cave one night and went out to explore the world. At some point, the bat touched another animal. Like a raccoon or opossum or dog. And when they touched, that animal got the virus that was on the bat's fur."

"Oh no!"

"Then that animal - let's say it was a raccoon - that raccoon with the virus went home and slept in its little den with its family.

And guess what happened next?"

"I don't know."

"Remember, I said it's extra contagious."

"Oh, its family got sick!"

"Yes," her mother said, "And then other animals too. Until one day, one of those infected animals got caught by a human. In a trap or something."

Ruthie gasped.

"Whoever caught that animal sold it to a market, kind of like a grocery store, that sells raw fish and meat. But it also sold living animals - snakes, cats, scorpions, all kinds of things. While the raccoon with the virus was there, what do you think happened?"

"The other animals got sick!"

"Yes, and not just the other animals, the raw meat and fish there probably got infected too. It was only a matter of time before that virus spread to the humans at the market. Maybe someone bought a cat from the market or took home some fish to cook."

Ruthie nodded.

"Let's say a lady, we'll call her Ming Li, bought some pork from the market. She went home with her pork and made dumplings for her family. Do you know what a dumpling is?"

"I think so."

"Well, over the next few days her family started to feel a little sick. They started to cough, maybe got fevers. Ming Li coughed while she did Tai Chi with her friends in the morning. Ming Li's husband coughed among the people he farmed with. Their child went to school and sneezed on his friends as he sat at his desk doing math. And then, guess what happened to Ming Li's friends, her husband's coworkers, and her child's classmates?"

"Momma, they got sick, too!"

"That's right."

"Viruses are really smart to make people cough and sneeze," Ruthie said, "That way they keep spreading."

"Exactly. You're a very smart girl. So, after their friends and coworkers and classmates got the virus, many of them spread it to their families. It spread mainly through coughing and sneezing, but sometimes even just breathing. Before long, the virus spread to the whole city where the market was, a city called Wuhan. Now, Wuhan is a very crowded, very busy city. It has more people in it than any city in the United States. So, you can imagine, when you have that many people crowded together, how quickly that virus can spread.

"Now, in a busy city like that, there are lots of people traveling in and out, right? So, let's say just one of those people in Wuhan had to travel to Japan, a nearby country, to do business. The businessman goes to the airport with a cough. And he flies on an airplane for a few hours. And, of course, while on the airplane, he coughs a good bit. Maybe he sneezes. And all those germs float around throughout the airplane, in the air that a few hundred passengers are breathing. When the airplane lands, those hundreds of people go to their homes, workplaces, and schools, continuing the spread of the virus in the country of Japan."

"Oh, so that happened over and over?"

"That's right, spreading to countries all over the world."

"Even America?"

"Especially America. And before long, governments all over

the world shut down airports to try and stop the virus."

"But that didn't work?"

"No, because by that point the virus was already everywhere."

"So, what did they do?"

"After that didn't work, the government said that everyone had to stay home. People had to either stop working or work from home. Mommy and Daddy weren't able to go to work for a while. That was meant to keep it from spreading more. Other countries did the same thing."

"Did that stop the virus?"

"It slowed it down, but not even that stopped it. Then scientists all over the world developed vaccines to try and prevent people from getting infected."

"Oh, that's good!"

"Yes, but COVID was a very smart virus, and found ways to change itself enough so that the vaccines didn't work that well. These are called variants."

"Vari-ants," Ruthie repeated.

"Other things were done too. People wore masks, people tried not to stand too close to each other or have too many friends together at once. That kind of thing."

"But it kept spreading."

"Yes. It spread all over the planet and was nearly impossible to stop, even though the smartest and most powerful people in the world were trying to stop it. It's hard to say how many people died from it, maybe millions. That's how your Great Aunt Margaret died."

"Wow," Ruthie said quietly. "Airports. Governments.

Mommy and Daddy's jobs. Aunt Margaret. Millions of people. It really did rule the world, didn't it?"

"In a way, yes. You can see now why your teacher said that."

Ruthie nodded. "And all that from a teeny tiny virus on a cute little bat," she said, staring at her thumb.

Questions

1. What is this story and parable reflecting about the nature of the gospel?

2. How is the kingdom like a virus? Like a pandemic?

3. Read the parable of the leaven (Matt. 13:33). How are Jesus' original metaphors for the kingdom (mustard seed and leaven) provocative?

4. In this story, a tiny bat is considered to have started the pandemic. What is the tiny "mustard seed" from which the kingdom has grown (see also John 12:24)?

5. How has the world been unsuccessful in preventing the advancement of the kingdom?

6. How is the kingdom still growing in ways that are small in the eyes of the world?

THE PARABLE OF THE GROWING SEED
Mark 4:26-29

"The kingdom of God is as if a man should scatter seed on the ground. He sleeps and rises night and day, and the seed sprouts and grows; he knows not how. The earth produces by itself, first the blade, then the ear, then the full grain in the ear. But when the grain is ripe, at once he puts in the sickle, because the harvest has come."

Birdie

"TELL YOU WHAT, RUBY. You help me in the garden, and afterwards we'll go get ice cream."

"OK, Birdie!" Ruby said, leaping up from the couch.

"Go get your boots," Birdie said. Ruby skipped to the spare room to her overnight bag. Birdie called, "And get your little jacket too. It's cool out this morning."

"Got it!" Ruby called back. She came back thirty seconds later, wearing her favorite butterfly jacket, complete with wings and antennae, and her polka dot rubber boots. "Ready," she said, jumping to a halt by the door.

"Goodness," Birdie said. "It takes your grandma thirty minutes just to put on her shoes. You're a hasty little thing. I've barely had time to blink."

Ruby smiled and tugged on her arm. "Let's go, Birdie!"

"Hang on now," Birdie said, "I've got to get my tools and apron. Now, where did I put them at the end of last season?"

Ruby sighed.

"Oh, I bet they're in the garage," Birdie said, turning around slowly. "Come along, you've got better eyes than your Birdie."

They went into the garage and Birdie turned on the light. Ruby immediately saw the gardening apron hanging on a hook on the wall, its pockets stuffed with tools. She ran over and tugged on it. "Here it is!" she said.

"Thank you, dear." Birdie walked to it and took it off the wall. She brushed off the cobwebs and wrapped it around herself.

"I wish I had one," Ruby said. "You have an extra one for me?"

"Oh, honey. I don't, but if you like gardening with me maybe we'll get you one soon."

"Can we get one today?"

"Not today. Soon. I'll let you use my tools though. Look, see this little box here? You can carry the seeds in it."

"Alright," Ruby said.

"Let's go get the seeds. They're back inside." They went back into the house. Birdie opened a drawer in the kitchen. "Now," she said under her breath, "Where did I put them?"

"Ready, Birdie?"

"Hold your horses," she said, opening a few more drawers. "Oh, you know what, I put them in the pantry." She walked across the kitchen into the pantry. "Here they are. Bring that box over here." She loaded it with various packs of seeds. "Alright, little one. Now we can go."

Ruby ran to the door and opened it, leaping outside. Sitting on a padded bench, Birdie hummed while she took off her slippers and slid her feet into her boots. Then she walked outside, closing the door behind her.

"You're right, it *is* cold," Ruby said. "It feels like winter."

"It is winter, baby girl."

"Maybe we should have cookies and milk instead of ice cream." Ruby looked at Birdie, who nodded.

"Maybe a slice a pie."

Ruby asked, "So you can have a garden in winter?"

"Well, you can *plant* a garden in winter. As long as spring is close."

"I didn't know that."

"Well, it doesn't really start to grow good until it warms up and the sun shines longer in the day." Birdie opened the little wooden gate to her garden and Ruby followed her in.

"What's the point of planting them now then?"

"We're just getting a head start. It takes them a while to wake up. No matter when you plant them, the seeds like to just sit in the ground for a while."

"Huh? Doing what?"

Birdie laughed. "Beats me! Your Birdie's got a green thumb but I'm no botanist. I just like to plant my own food and see it grow." She walked over to one of her three raised beds, Ruby a step behind her. "Now, we're going to start on this side and plant in rows going that way, longways. Here, hold out your little paw." She poured out some seeds into Ruby's hand. "Those are cabbage seeds. You take a couple of them, like this, and put them down in the earth like that. And then just cover them up with a little blanket of dirt to keep them warm. After that, we move over a couple of feet and do it again."

After Ruby had made a row she said, "Birdie, I got a bunch of extra seeds. Should I plant those, too?"

"Oh, thank you honey. No. Give 'em here. I'll save those for next year." She poured them back into the seed packet.

"Ok, well, what's next?"

"Let's do a row of spinach and a row of broccoli. Then the next bed we'll do tomaters and peppers." Ruby giggled.

After they finished the two beds Ruby said, "What goes in the third bed?"

"Oh, I'll leave that one empty for a while. That's for the taters, but it's too early."

"Why can't we plant them now?"

"I don't know. I tried this early once before and they went bad. They just rotted in the ground." She sighed and wiped the dirt off her hands onto her apron.

"What now?"

"They need a drink of water now. Seeds get real thirsty all a sudden when you put 'em in the ground. Don't ask me why. Can you go turn on that faucet by the house? Then drag that hose over here and turn it on. We'll give 'em a little drink."

Ruby skipped to the house and came back with the hose. Birdie said, "You move like lightning, you know that?" Ruby smiled and watered the beds.

"Alright, they should be satisfied 'til tomorrah," Birdie said. "Can you turn it off?" Ruby ran, turned it off, and came back. "You sure saved my back and knees a lot of work today," Birdie said, giving her a hug.

Ruby smiled. "I thought it was fun. Think they'll be ready in the morning?"

Birdie laughed. "Ready! Not everything grows as fast as you. Child, most of this won't be ready for months, some of it not 'til summer."

"Summer!" Ruby said. "That's for*ever*."

Birdie shrugged her shoulders. "Just the way it works. If you want it quick, go to the grocery store."

"Why does it take so long?"

"Probably to teach patience to hasty little girls." Birdie laughed. "Like I said, don't ask me. Gardeners aren't scientists. They just grow things."

"So, what do we do while we wait? How do we make sure they grow?"

"Listen, I'll tell you a little secret about gardening. The kind of thing only old grannies like me know. Are you listening?" Ruby nodded. "Are you really listening?"

"Yes, Birdie."

Quiet and serious, Birdie leaned forward and said, "A gardener doesn't grow nothing. Mother Earth - she's the real gardener. She does all the heavy lifting. We're just here to assist. To serve. To give her what she asks for - a daily drink of water, a patch of dirt, and a warm, sunny place to grow. That's it. Mother Earth is easy to please."

"Couldn't we do something to make it grow faster? Or bigger?"

"Sure, if you want to destroy it. Listen, the best way to ruin a garden is to force it to do something it's not meant to - that's what's wrong with people these days. Let the earth decide what size things need to be. And how long they need to take. The earth knows way better than us how to grow things."

"What about weeds? And rabbits? Or bugs? And do plants ever get sick?"

"Well," Birdie stopped and thought for a second. She shook

her head. "Maybe next time we'll talk about that. Just remember today's lesson. A gardener's job is just to give the earth what it asks for. Once you do that, you sit back and watch it do its thing. It's the earth that does the growing."

"What do we do now?"

"Now we warm ourselves up with a slice a pie and wash it down with a glass of milk. Then your old Birdie is going to read in her chair, maybe doze for a bit. And while we snack and read and rest our eyes, guess what?"

"What?"

"The earth is going to do its thing, baby girl."

Questions

1. Similar to the farmer in the parable, Birdie is unaware of the biological processes that take place to make plants grow, yet she appears to be a successful gardener. How does this relate to the Christian life, and how does it make room for trust?

2. Birdie makes the point that the gardener does not do the growing but assists and serves the earth as it does all the work. How does this relate to spiritual growth and ministry? How does it allow us to rest?

3. What major difference do you notice between Ruby and Birdie? How does this serve the point of the parable?

4. How does this parable speak to our desire to be productive and efficient?

The Parable of the Barren Fig Tree
Luke 13:6-9

"A man had a fig tree planted in his vineyard, and he came seeking fruit on it and found none. And he said to the vinedresser, 'Look, for three years now I have come seeking fruit on this fig tree, and I find none. Cut it down. Why should it use up the ground?' And he answered him, 'Sir, let it alone this year also, until I dig around it and put on manure. Then if it should bear fruit next year, well and good; but if not, you can cut it down.'"

The Third Option

"IT'S TIME FOR HIM TO COME HOME," Don said. "Vick can't even maintain a 2.0 GPA. He's dropped so many classes, it's going to take him another five years before he's done. If he even finishes."

"I know," said Joy, "I know you're right, but what's he going to do when he comes home?"

"Get a job!"

"But what job? Don't you want your son to have a college education? His future would be so limited."

"Anything is better than him using up our hard-earned money loafing around at the fraternity," Don said. "I don't care if Vick's a butcher, a fireman or a ... oh, what do you call it? They drive people around ..."

"Taxicab driver?"

"No."

"Uber driver?"

"No."

"Ok, well, I know what you're saying."

"A *chauffeur*! That's it. The point is there's plenty of good jobs for someone without a college degree. I'm serious, Joy, I'm done. Not another semester. Really, what are we teaching him by letting him sit on his butt all day playing video games and drinking beer?"

"I'm with you," Joy said, "No one is winning the way things are."

"OK, so we've agreed. He's coming home."

Joy hesitated.

Don continued, "He'll live with us, get a job, pay rent. It will be good for him. Maybe he'll grow up."

"But, Don, it would be hell for him. Don't you think he would be miserable? I'm not saying he doesn't deserve it, but he would want to die living back here at home while all his friends are back at college."

"Tough! He lost his chance!"

"I don't know," she said.

"Give me one reason we should expect anything to change? One reason that his grades will go up, that he will start going to class and stop partying."

"I know, I know."

"It's been an absolutely fruitless endeavor. A waste of money and time. I think he's worse off for having gone, I really do. Why did we expect anything different? He wasn't ready for this kind of freedom, and we knew it."

Joy reached over and put her hand on his to calm him down. "I'm just not sure that's what's best for him. Maybe there's a third option," she said.

"A third option? Like?"

She thought for a moment. "What if we gave him some consequences?"

"OK, like what?"

"We could stop paying for the fraternity. That way he wouldn't be able to waste all his time there. I'm sure it would cut down on the partying too."

"Alright, not bad. That might help. It's going to take more than that though."

She paused and closed her eyes. "I say we pay for housing and tuition. Food and fun he'll have to pay for himself with a job."

Don nodded. "I like it, keep going."

"We could take his truck from him. He spends half his time driving around with friends."

"Right, but how would he get to school?" Don said.

"We could make him move out of his apartment and move onto campus."

"Ah! In a dorm. Perfect. That might actually get his lazy butt to class. Where else would he have to go? He'd be stuck on campus all the time. I think you might have something, Joy. Make him pay for wasting our time and money. That'll teach him."

"No, we're not making him pay. This isn't punitive."

"Call it what you want, a little suffering can go a long way."

"I think the word you're looking for is 'discipline.'"

"Right, right. Discipline."

"I agree though. Discipline involves suffering, no doubt about it. But it's very carefully measured, and it's just the right kind. And it's only because we love him. He won't see it that way, though."

"Of course not. He's going to hate it. And he'll hate us. You know that, right?"

"Oh, I know. He'll tell us we're cruel and we're ruining his life. He'll be mad at us for a while, probably not speak to us. But he'll get over it. Eventually. Maybe one day he'll even thank us for it."

Don laughed. "Wouldn't that be something?"

"I do feel for him, though. We're basically removing all the fun from his life. And really most of his friends, too." Joy started to tear up. "It's not going to be easy to watch. He's going to be so lonely. Bored. Depressed, probably. But it's just for a season. When it's all said and done, I really think it will make for a much more fruitful college experience."

"If he *receives* the discipline, it will. I'm not as confident as you, though. I'm not so sure he'll respond the way we're hoping. What if it doesn't do any good?"

"It'll just prove he's not fit for college."

"And then?"

"Then he's coming home. And if he does respond well and his grades go up this year, he can get some of his privileges back. At least, the ones that we think he's ready for."

Don reached over and gave Joy's shoulder a gentle squeeze. "You going to call him? Or you want me to?"

"I love to see my boy happy, almost more than anything, but his good comes first." She sighed and picked up her phone. "I'll call him."

Questions

1. In what way is Vick "barren?" Biblically speaking, what does it mean for someone to be a "barren fig tree?" In what way was this the case for Israel in Jesus' day?

2. Describe the nature of the discipline Vick will receive from his parents. How does this reflect the discipline God gives to his children?

3. What would it mean for Vick to "receive" his discipline? How should the child of God receive his /her discipline?

4. Why would it be unloving for Vick's parents to allow him to continue as he is? Similarly, why would it be unloving for God to let his children remain fruitless?

5. Discipline is hard and unpleasant by design. How is it also gracious?

6. How does Vick's mother feel about having to give discipline? How does she reflect the heart of God, especially as displayed in Lamentations 3:33?

THE PARABLE OF THE SOWER
Matthew 13:3-9

"A sower went out to sow. And as he sowed, some seeds fell along the path, and the birds came and devoured them. Other seeds fell on rocky ground, where they did not have much soil, and immediately they sprang up, since they had no depth of soil, but when the sun rose they were scorched. And since they had no root, they withered away. Other seeds fell among thorns, and the thorns grew up and choked them. Other seeds fell on good soil and produced grain, some a hundredfold, some sixty, some thirty. He who has ears, let him hear."

A Mother's Love

A MOTHER. THAT'S ALL ALICE HAD EVER WANTED TO BE. She had never been very career-driven like some of her friends. She worked, but it was only ever a way to underwrite what Alice believed to be her true calling, motherhood.

Having had friends who'd endured miscarriages and infertility, Alice knew what a gift she had been given and often rejoiced in it. She had three children in five years and then, at forty - surprise - a fourth child. Two boys, two girls, in that order. Her husband Allen, a good man, often felt like he came second to the children. Although that was in many ways true, she loved him dearly.

Pete came first. Alpha Pete, they called him. They joked that he had come out of the womb in charge. As he grew, he never lost his Alpha. Outgoing, extraverted, loud, and easily angered, Pete got a large share of the attention in the home. Although Pete was headstrong and challenging, Alice and Allen gave him the love and discipline he needed, as best they could, believing that with the right care he could become a strong leader of a man.

Then there was Eric, a walking brain. From early on, what he lacked in courage and conviction, Eric made up for in craft and precision. Eric was smart enough to avoid getting caught at most things and was therefore considered "the good one." He especially enjoyed provoking his siblings into trouble while avoiding it himself. Although his parents often wondered what was "going on in that brain of his" and felt like he kept them at a distance, they believed in and encouraged his gifts, looking forward to what he would become.

Third came Georgia, whom the doctor had pronounced at birth - Alice would often repeat - 'the most beautiful child he'd ever delivered.' Indeed, Georgia was a very pretty little girl, who received compliments wherever she went in public. As Alice put it, Georgia had her father Allen 'wrapped around her little finger,' which bothered Alice but did not keep her from giving her full love and attention to her daughter.

Lastly, five years later came Bridget, who was instantly nicknamed BB - Baby Bridget. It's hard to know what to say about BB; there simply wasn't much to her. Of course, her parents would never have said such a thing, and she was loved and nurtured just like the others. Among her siblings, however, BB often felt invisible, and perhaps with good reason, for in the midst of the busyness and angst of their teenage years, her brothers and sister virtually forgot her. Even so, despite her plainness and apparent lack of gifting, her parents considered her a delightful surprise and treasured her.

Alice watched them grow with mixed feelings. She loved them, and therefore rejoiced to see them growing up into their own unique personalities. Seeing her many sacrifices bear fruit in their lives was one of the most gratifying things of her life. And yet, she also grieved to see them grow, because the older they became, the less they needed her. She was also fearful because her love for them, necessarily, left her vulnerable towards them. And she knew that children have a way of breaking their parents' hearts as nothing and no one else can.

In his teenage years, Pete was, unsurprisingly, a star athlete. What he lacked in academic ability he made up for in charisma. He was popular and magnetic in personality. Also a bit of a hothead, he made a number of enemies on the ballfield and was easily drawn into fights at parties. His mother was relieved when, despite his grades, he received a full-ride college scholarship for baseball.

Eric succeeded marvelously in his youth and, though very different from his older brother, he was popular and omni-talented, succeeding in sports, the arts, and academics. Yet, he did his best to fly under the radar, avoiding both the spotlight as well as trouble. He was polite and smiled often, but, just as when he was little, he never seemed fully present. Alice felt he withheld himself from her. Even so, Eric was an easy-going, respectful young man with a bright future, and they invested in him in every way possible. He easily got a scholarship to the state university, where he was thankful to finally live away from the observation and rule of his parents.

Georgia. Oh, Georgia. She was a whirlwind, in both wonderful and overwhelming ways. She could brighten the home with joy the moment she walked in the door. And yet, she brought more drama to the home than the rest of the family combined. The volatility of her emotions kept everyone on edge, all of them bracing for the next moment of eruption. Ever since elementary school, Georgia had a revolving door of boyfriends, who increasingly consumed her thoughts. Alice tried, with as much patience and wisdom as possible, to address Georgia's choice of clothing, which embarrassed her mother and struck her father with horror. They had their concerns but believed and hoped that a private Christian college education would help her grow into a mature woman.

Lastly, little BB. BB was the eternal "baby" of the family. Even physically, she was a late bloomer. "Have you seen the baby?" her mom would ask her father, even when BB was almost a teenager. BB was only twelve when Georgia left for college, which left the home incredibly quiet and, for everyone, a little boring. Her parents, still searching for some kind of talent to invest in or something exceptional to praise, would ask her, "BB, would you like to take some art classes? Or do gymnastics?" BB would smile and say, "If you want me to, Momma." Her grades were passing but unremarkable. She had a few friends, but no best friends. And by the time she went to the local community college, she had never been kissed, something that left her with a bit of shame, especially when she compared herself to Georgia. BB continued to live at home, which brought Alice a great deal of comfort, extending the season of motherhood, but this also concerned her. "I'm just praying she finds her way," Alice would tell Allen.

Unfortunately for Alice and Allen, the years of college and beyond held a great deal of heartbreak. As most parents naturally do, they blamed themselves for the tragic mistakes of their children, but in fact they had nothing to do with it. Just the opposite, their parenting, though not perfect, was full of wisdom and love, intentional and personal. The problem was not with their parenting, but with their children, who rejected everything their parents had sown into their lives in their formative years.

The first tragedy came in Pete's junior year of college. He had been suspended from the baseball team for flunking several classes, and his scholarship was on the line. When he found this out, rather than accepting the discipline and showing up to class or turning to his parents for help, Pete got on his motorcycle and sped down the interstate to blow off some steam - a habit he'd developed in college. The faster he went, the more it eased his frustration. A policeman clocked him at 135 mph, but was not able to stop him before it was too late. Less than a mile later, Pete slammed into the back of an 18 wheeler, which had slowed for traffic. He was thrown from his motorcycle and somehow survived; however, he was not wearing a helmet and therefore suffered a broken neck and severe brain damage. After many months of surgeries and convalescence in the hospital, he was placed in a nursing home, where, his parents hope, Alpha Pete will be renewed, learning to walk and speak again.

The second tragedy came when Eric was a sophomore in college, although the seeds were planted for it long before in all the secrets he'd kept from his parents. Alice and Allen first became aware of his secretive life when he was busted his freshman year for growing psychedelic mushrooms in his dorm room closet. They were shocked, hurt, and deeply shaken - the first hint that their wonder boy was not what he seemed. But his grades were fine, so they let him stay. They wept hot tears of regret over this decision when, the following year, Eric's girlfriend found him lying on the kitchen floor of his apartment, his face blue and mouth gurgling. Eric had overdosed on fentanyl, and though he survived, he was not able to finish school but went to a rehab in California. He has remained on the west coast ever since and has continued to wrestle with drugs and alcohol. His parents grieve to see his brilliant mind now withered by the paranoia and delusion of his addictions and pray that he would somehow find the will to return to his roots.

At least with Georgia, her parents had some foresight of the sorrow that would come to them. The older Georgia got, the more risky and unhealthy her relationships became. She brought the first few boyfriends home from college to meet her parents, but each time it was so disastrous that everyone was relieved when she stopped bringing them home. It broke Allen's heart to see his daughter's beauty choked by sensuality and licentiousness. Ultimately, after not hearing from her for weeks, Georgia's roommate called and informed them that Georgia had eloped with a married man. Anticipating their disapproval, she had cut off contact with her parents. Her rejection of them hurt even more than any of her poor choices, but they chose not to close their heart towards her, in the event that she chose to turn over a new leaf and come home.

Of course, having experienced these tragic losses with her first three children, Alice could not help but brace herself for tragedy with BB. At the same time, Alice began to notice a few things that distinguished her from her siblings. When BB made a mistake, for instance, she either confessed or readily admitted to it when confronted, accepting whatever consequences came with it. When BB had a problem, she didn't hide it but came to her parents for help - "Mom, can we talk?" And even when she finally began to make close friends and, finally, a boyfriend in college, her parents remained, as she put it, her "people." BB finished an associate's degree at the local community college and got a job as a dental hygienist. Still living at home, she did her best to comfort and encourage her parents as they carried the sorrows of their first three children. BB married in her late twenties, moving into a house a few streets over from her parents, where she lives now and keeps a little vegetable garden. Other than thanksgiving for BB's quiet, abundant life, Alice's main prayer is that her daughter would be fruitful and multiply - meaning, of course, grandchildren.

Although BB's life was not exceptional by any typical definition of greatness, Alice increasingly felt that she had underestimated her daughter. She had always called BB 'a late bloomer' but realized now that she was mistaken. Alice had always looked for the power, intelligence, and beauty that her first three children possessed and had missed the fact that, all along, BB was flourishing.

Questions

1. Describe Alice's feelings for her children. How does this reflect God's heart for humanity?

2. How do the first three children and their mistakes resemble the failed seeds in the parable? What hope is there for them?

3. Do you identify with any of the seeds and soils? What should you do if you think you're not "in good soil"?

4. In what ways did BB flourish? Why had Alice not seen it?

5. Give a definition or description of success or prosperity, according to the world. How does that differ from the way Scripture describes a flourishing human being?

PART 4
PARABLES OF THE END

THE PARABLE OF THE WICKED TENANTS
Luke 20:9-16

"A man planted a vineyard and let it out to tenants and went into another country for a long while. When the time came, he sent a servant to the tenants, so that they would give him some of the fruit of the vineyard. But the tenants beat him and sent him away empty-handed. And he sent another servant. But they also beat and treated him shamefully, and sent him away empty-handed. And he sent yet a third. This one also they wounded and cast out. Then the owner of the vineyard said, 'What shall I do? I will send my beloved son; perhaps they will respect him.' But when the tenants saw him, they said to themselves, 'This is the heir. Let us kill him, so that the inheritance may be ours.' And they threw him out of the vineyard and killed him. What then will the owner of the vineyard do to them? He will come and destroy those tenants and give the vineyard to others."

Beautiful Boy

WHEN ROBERT FITZGERALD SR. WAS IN HIS MID-THIRTIES, he inherited a tract of undeveloped, wooded land, close to 1200 acres. For many years leading up to this, Robert had the same conversation with his father. They had it one last time when his father was on his deathbed.

"Son, about the land."

"Yes, the land," Robert said with a knowing smile.

"Your great grandfather bought that land from Thomas Jefferson himself after the Louisiana Purchase. Ever since, that land has been a Fitzgerald family heirloom. It's the best savings account in existence. It's immune to inflation. It replenishes itself. It's secure from thieves and moths and rust. Besides," he said, pausing for effect. Robert knew his next words verbatim. His father looked to the right and left and leaned close to Robert. "They're *virgin* hardwoods," he said quietly, "Never been touched by a man since the good Lord brought them forth from the ground."

"I understand."

"Don't dare sell it. Only if you are on the brink of starvation, you hear?"

"Yes sir."

His father nodded and sat back in bed peacefully, as if his mind had been eased of a great anxiety.

Several years before his father had passed, Robert had lost his wife, leaving him with Junior, their only son, whom he felt entirely unprepared to raise on his own. Although the death of his father added to his grief, it also birthed in him an idea, a way to both honor his father's memory and help him to raise Junior.

Robert began to make plans for the land. Not, of course, to sell it. A lifelong hunter, he wanted to make a deer hunting lease out of it. He felt like this would make some use and profit from the land while it appreciated in a way that did not go against his father's wishes. The land instantly became Robert's pet project, and Junior took to it better than he had ever expected. From the time Junior was ten, any weekend they could spare, they headed to the woods and camped out, setting up a tent and building a fire to keep warm and cook over. The land became a kind of sacred bond between the two that made it possible for them to know each other in the fullness of father and son. "You're a fine young man, Junior," Robert would often tell him, "A beautiful boy."

Robert moved slowly, intending for the project to last for the rest of Junior's childhood. Besides the many years of laboring together, they spent countless nights talking under the stars, sharing the secrets of their hearts, telling stories, made-up and true. While they mapped out the land and cleared the trails,

Robert found he could talk about the past: the history of the place, his childhood, and, especially, Junior's mother. At the same time they took notes on the tracks and trails and sightings of deer, Robert counseled Junior through the drama and angst of his teenage years. Their relationship became bound up with the place. Sometimes, lying awake in the tent next to his sleeping son, Robert would become aware how much he had come to love the boy, and he would grow afraid.

The amount of initial work and upkeep was substantial, and Robert often brought friends and their children along to help. Every so often while he and Junior were out in the woods, he would come across the neighbors, a man named Whit and his sons Mudd and Porkpie. Although uneducated, foul-mouthed, and heavy drinkers, they had a knowledge of the land that far surpassed his own. They could predict the weather and read the woods and game trails in ways that approached a sixth sense. They were attentive to Junior, teaching him how to set up ingenious traps for small game and how to make his own fishing pole and primitive bow. Whit became like an uncle to Junior, his boys like cousins. Robert began to rely on them for their advice and knowledge of the land. They helped him place and set up blinds and stands and deer feeders throughout the woods. It did bother him that they used his land so freely without asking, and apparently had done so for many years, but they were so helpful he decided to let it go.

Over the years Robert saved up everything he could spare. Finally, using his savings and a small equity loan on the land, he had a dozen simple cabins built, plus a larger one for himself and

Junior. The neighbors offered to build the cabins for half the price of the contractor in town, to which Robert gladly agreed. He was pleased but surprised at the quality of their work, given the dilapidated home they lived in down the road. When the cabins were completed, it seemed only natural to hire Whit as the lease manager and Mudd and Porkpie as the groundskeepers. In addition to a salary, they were allowed use of one of the cabins and were given formal permission to hunt and use the land.

Finally, fifteen years after beginning the project, Robert got his lease license and began accepting hunters for the upcoming season. That summer he and Junior, now a twenty-five-year-old man, brought potential hunters out to the land, showing the trails and stands and cabins. There were many who had waited for years for the place to open officially and some who had already hunted it here and there. Thus, the lease quickly met its capacity of hunters.

Bow season opened October 1. Robert didn't care much for bowhunting and did not mind missing the first weekend, so he let a friend stay in his cabin. Besides, he thought, Whit and his boys would be there to take care of things. He waited eagerly to hear the results of opening day, imagining a flood of congratulatory calls. Yet, to his surprise, no one called. In fact, he received emails from two people withdrawing from the lease and requesting a refund. One of them refused even to talk to him. The other answered his call.

"Those rednecks you got running the place are going to ruin it, Rob," he said.

"What do you mean?" Robert said. "What did they do?"

"For one, they partied all night, I mean partied hard.

Drinking, hollering, cussing, fighting. At about two in the morning, I went outside and asked if they could quiet down. You know what they did? One of those brothers took a pistol out of his drawers and fired it in the air. *Bang! Bang! Bang!* Then he said, 'I'll be loud as I want, partner. You're on my land.'"

"What? You're kidding."

"No sir. I wish I was. And that's not all. The next morning when it was finally time to get out of bed and into the woods, I went outside, and my four-wheeler was nowhere in sight. Just plain gone."

"You think they stole it?"

"You got a better explanation?"

"Unbelievable, I'm so sorry. I'll call them right now and sort this out. I swear, I'll get to the bottom of this. I'll get back to you."

Robert immediately tried to call Whit but could not reach him. He tried again on Wednesday but still did not get an answer. He planned to go out to the deer lease that weekend and personally confront Whit and his sons. Unfortunately, an urgent issue came up at work on Thursday, and Robert was asked to travel over the weekend to meet a client. He flew out, vexed and uneasy.

All Friday while Robert worked, the situation gnawed at him. Also, it bothered him that he still hadn't heard back from the other hunter who withdrew, a close friend. *It was probably just a misunderstanding,* he told himself. *Boys being boys.* He hadn't wanted to get Junior worked up, but by Saturday morning he was so uneasy about it all, he excused himself from a meeting with a client and called his son. Now a hulk of a man, Junior was a forester living in a small town not far from the family land. Junior was concerned, too, but unsurprised.

"You know them," Junior said. "They're not the sharpest. They just need some things spelled out for them. Managing the place has probably gone to their heads a little."

Robert said, "I shouldn't have hired them. I had my doubts. I might need to find someone else to manage it."

"I'll do it," Junior said. "If they don't work out, I'll manage it for you."

"No, son."

"Why not? I work in the area anyway. I know the place as well as you do. It'd be an honor. I'd love to do it."

"No, not yet at least. I need to go talk with them and get to the bottom of things."

"I'll go talk with them," said Junior.

"No. Something is off. I've got a feeling something's not right."

"Listen, I'm not going to pick a fight. I just want them to remember they don't own the place. Plus, maybe there's more to the story. I'll go visit with them just like I have a thousand times."

"Just wait until I get back. We'll go together."

Junior kept pressing. "Just a visit. To put an eye on things. I won't even stay the night."

Robert was quiet and felt uneasy. "I don't know."

"Dad, they've known me for what, fifteen years? What are you so worried about? They'd never hurt me. They're like family. They've always been respectful of me."

Robert sighed. "Fine. Just promise me you'll be careful."

"Promise," Junior said. "Just a quick visit tomorrow afternoon. I'll call you as soon as I leave."

Talking with Junior had relieved some of Robert's distress. He was able to sleep a little better that night in the hotel and was able to finish up his work by lunch on Sunday. That afternoon, he finally heard from the other hunter who had withdrawn from the lease.

"What were you thinking, Rob?"

"What?"

"You got terrorists managing your lease, that's what."

"What happened?" Robert grew alarmed, thinking of Junior.

"First, I get out there Saturday morning and those two brothers tell me I have to pay a $500 fee for my friend I brought with me. I pay it - whatever. But I didn't like the sight of those two. Look like meth heads to me, black teeth and all. Anyway, I go out there that evening and kill a beautiful eight point. I mean, a prize-winning buck. It's getting dark so my buddy helps me track it, and then we bring it back to the camp to dress it and clean it. Then, that old man - what's his name?"

"Whit."

"Whit tells me I should have dressed it out in the woods. He says there's a cleaning fee for dressing it in the camp. 'That'll be another five hunnard,' he says. I tell him not to worry, I'll clean up after myself, and that it was too dark to gut it in the woods. I tell him I've never heard of a rule like that. You know what he says?"

"What?"

"He says, 'This is my lease, boy. I make the rules. Pay up or get lost.'"

"I tell him, 'This is Rob's lease. I'll take it up with *him*.' Next thing I know one of his sons jumped me. Hit me right over the head with a shovel. Surprised that fat son of a gun didn't break my neck. My buddy was about to stand up to them, but they pulled a knife on him. Then they walked off, dragging the deer behind them by the antlers. We got out of there quick."

"This is outrageous! I can't believe it."

"I know it ain't your fault but I've been mad at you, Rob. Took me a week before I was up for talking. I'm out of the lease. And by the way, if I weren't your friend, I'd be suing you right now."

"I'm so sorry. I'll take care of this, I promise. Dear God, I wish I would've known sooner," Robert said. He felt betrayed and was furious with Whit. Far beyond anger, however, he was alarmed for his son and felt helpless. After hanging up, he immediately called Junior to stop him from going, but Junior did not answer.

That same afternoon, after all the weekend hunters had gone home, Junior drove out to the deer lease. Whit saw him stop at the gate to open it. He turned to Mudd and Porkpie. "Look who it is, boys. The Crown Prince." Whit looked around at the cabins and beyond to the woods. He stroked his gray beard and smiled. "You know what happens to an inher'tance when there ain't no heir?"

"Huh," said Mudd.

"It's fair game."

"What'chu mean, Deddy?" said Porkpie.

"I mean it's time to take what's ours for good. To claim the throne. Ever'thing's fallin' right into place." Whit grunted. "Fetch my forty-five, boy."

Sunday evening, Robert had still not heard from Junior. He laid awake that night in fear, worse case scenarios replaying themselves in his mind. He had not heard from Junior by the next morning either and called the police in a panic, asking them to investigate. "My boy is missing. My big, beautiful boy." He told them the story. "You've got to find him." Robert got on a flight home later that morning. That afternoon, not long after he stepped off the airplane, Robert received a phone call.

"This is Kevin Mitchell from the state coroner's office. Is this Robert Fitzgerald, Sr.?"

"Yes. Yes it is, have you found my boy? Have you found Junior?"

"You're the next of kin for Robert Fitzgerald, Jr.?"

"Yes, yes, is he OK?"

"Are you sitting down, sir?"

Robert sat down on a bench in the airport lobby. "Yes."

Robert heard the coroner take a breath. "Last night police investigators found your son's body in the woods, not too far off Highway 91. The presumed cause of death was a gunshot to the head."

"No," Robert said.

"I'm very sorry for your loss, sir."

"No," he said again. The coroner was quiet. The many nights beneath the stars long ago passed before his mind. "No, not my boy," he said, choking on his words. He saw Junior as a boy, crouched beside the fire, tossing twigs onto it and blowing into the coals. He saw him as a lanky teenager, climbing into a tree stand in the rain. He saw his son as he last saw him, more of a man than himself, a rifle slung over his broad shoulders. "My big, beautiful boy." He saw him dead in the woods off Highway 71.

The coroner continued. "There is a murder investigation underway, although I am not able to provide details at this time. We've identified several suspects and are currently in pursuit of them. We hope to have them in custody soon."

Robert's chest heaved up and down. He could not catch his breath. Unable to speak, the noise that did come out sounded more like a wounded fawn than a human.

The coroner waited patiently. After a while he said, "I'm sorry again for your loss."

"I'll come help you find them. It's 1200 acres. You won't find them without me."

"Mr. Fitzgerald, please leave the investigation to the police."

"I know the land," Robert said, still breathing heavily. "I know all their hiding places. You won't find them without me. Tell the investigators I'm on my way. I'm coming to help with the manhunt."

"I'd strongly advise you not to, Mr. Fitzgerald. Leave it to the professionals. Go home and get some rest. We'll call you when we know more. You have my word; we will see that justice is done."

"No sir, Mr. Coroner. It's not just justice. He went out there to rescue the land. His death can't be for nothing. I can't rest, not until Junior — *God bless him. . .*" Robert covered his face and was unable to speak for a while. He took a deep, ragged breath. "Not until I get our land back. For Junior's sake. It's all I've got left of him."

Questions

1. How does Robert's relationship with Junior provide a glimpse into the Father's love for the Son?

2. How do you see the wicked tenants reflected in Whit and his sons?

3. How does what happens to Junior help you see afresh the crucifixion of Jesus?

4. Likewise, how does it help you appreciate the resurrection?

5. At the heart of this parable is the tenants' seizing of the vineyard that does not belong to them. How does this encapsulate not just the life of Christ, but the entire history of humanity?

6. If this does reflect human history, who do Whitt, Mudd, and Porkpie represent? How does this shine new light on God's grace?

Subversive Stories

THE PARABLE OF THE NET
Matthew 13:47-50

"Again, the kingdom of heaven is like a net that was thrown into the sea and gathered fish of every kind. When it was full, men drew it ashore and sat down and sorted the good into containers but threw away the bad. So it will be at the end of the age. The angels will come out and separate the evil from the righteous and throw them into the fiery furnace. In that place there will be weeping and gnashing of teeth."

Jimbo and Gumbo

"HAND ME THEM PLIERS, GUMBO," said Jimbo, reaching his hand out. "Mine'r gone."

"Whaddya gimme for 'em?" said Gumbo, reaching into his tacklebox.

"I'll catch you a fish so big you'll wet your drawers."

"You got yourself a deal," said Gumbo, handing him the pliers. Jimbo reached over the side of the boat and corrected the curve of a hook that had been nearly bent straight. "Whatever it was bent a hook this bad's prolly big 'nough to do the trick."

"Reckon so," said Gumbo. "And smart 'nough not to stick around for a coupla' fish ticklers like us."

They continued to move quietly along the lake in their jon boat, one up front, one in the back with a trolling motor. Every six feet or so they would stop, and Gumbo, up front, would reach down with a hooked pole and pull up the trot line. They each had a five-gallon paint bucket full of bait fish to hook on the line.

"Gumbo, how much trot line you think we got out in this lake by now?" Jimbo said.

"Shoot," he said.

"Huh?"

"I bet we got a mile's worth," said Gumbo, his eyes wide.

"A mile!" said Jimbo, laughing and rocking the boat. "You lost your durn mind."

Gumbo, only slightly offended, said, "Well, let's hear your est'mate."

"Enough. We got enough, that's how much," he said.

Gumbo looked across the lake and thought for a moment. "A man can't argue with an answer like that. Enough," he repeated and laughed. "Don't know why you asked the question in the first place since you was already knowin' the answer."

"S'pose you got a point there," said Jimbo, putting his hand to the homemade tiller attached to the trolling motor. "Now, let's go check that line we set this mornin'." The jon boat turned and cruised silently through a series of stumps and entered open water. After crossing the channel, they reached a patch of trees about fifty feet from the bank.

"All right, let's see what's for dinner," Gumbo said, putting a glove on one hand. He reached his pole down into the water and drew up the black, braided trotline. A catfish thrashed the top of the water. "Open that Igloo, quick!" He grabbed the catfish with his gloved hand, removed the hook from its mouth, and threw it in the ice chest.

"Ain't too big," Jimbo said.

"Ain't too small, neither. He'll fry up just fine." They moved along a few feet and Gumbo raised the next hook. "Heck, I knew it," said Gumbo. "Hate these nasty dinosaurs."

"Snappin' turtle?"

"Yeah. If I hadn't forgot my .22, I'd shoot the son of a gun right here and now. Ain't no other way to kill 'em."

"Just leave it on the hook," Jimbo said, "If it's still livin' when we come back t'morra, I'll have my gun with me and take care of it."

"You got it boss." Gumbo paused. "You know, some people say you can eat 'em."

Jimbo laughed. "Oh, go right on ahead! Keep 'em. See how many fingers he gets first. And how many hours you reckon you gon' spen' crackin' that shell open?"

"I know. I jus' pickin'," said Gumbo, smiling. They continued down the trot line. The next was a small white perch. "What do you think, let 'em go?"

"Huh? They's good eatin', boy. My momma would'a skint you alive for sayin' less than that. Nothin' sweeter than a little perch."

Gumbo smiled and tossed it into the ice chest. He knew they always kept the perch. He just liked getting Jimbo riled up. The next few hooks were perch as well, which they kept.

They noticed the next catch thrashing at the top of the water. Before they got to it, Jimbo rubbed his hands together and said, "Largemouth."

Gumbo pulled it out of the water. The fish hung from the hook and spun slowly. "Would ya' look at that. Ain't she purty, Jimbo?"

"She sure is," said Jimbo. "She's a heifer too. Lay her out, lemme see her from head to toe."

Gumbo laid the fish out on top of the ice chest. "Lordy," he said. "Ain't that the purtiest set o' lips you ever saw on a bass? I could almost kiss 'em."

"Boy, put that fish in that ice chest 'fore you get yourself in trouble with your wife."

"Momma don't mind. Just sayin', that's the kind o' fish that gets a fella' up in the mornin'. Ain't every day you haul a fish that looks as good as it tastes." Gumbo put the bass in the ice chest and moved on finally. He tried to pull up the next hook. "Shoot, get over here," he said, straining. "Don't know what this is but it's gon' take all hands on deck." They pulled up the line, revealing the top half of a massive catfish.

"Look'a this lunker, Gumbo!"

"Shut up and help me!" They pulled it over the side of the boat where it flung itself around violently and growled. They both stepped back from it.

"Sooie! He ain' gon' fit in the chest!"

"No matter, jus' hold 'em down while I get the hook out his gullet." Gumbo took the pliers in his gloved hand and reached into its mouth, removing the hook. After he finished and flung the hook out, he sat back on the cushioned seat, soaked with lake water.

"Told ya I'd catch you a fish so big you'd wet your drawers," Jimbo said. They laughed together and shook the boat.

"Whew, I'm 'bout done. Let's finish up and get home," he said, still breathing hard. "Soon as I get my wits back." Finally, he said, "All right, last one." They moved forward and he pulled up the line a little. "Ah, shoulda known," he said. "Dadgum gar."

"Huh?"

"Alligator gar," said Gumbo loudly. "Can't never have a trot line with no gar. Get over here and take care of 'em. Evil, worthless creatures. Nothin' makes me doubt the Creator's wisdom like a gar." Jimbo came to the front of the boat with a machete and hacked at the top of the gar's head. When he was sure it was dead, Gumbo took it off the hook and let the corpse float away in the water.

"No pest worse than a gar," said Gumbo. "Trash fish if I ever saw one. Eatin' up all the beauties. Did ya' know if she's got eggs in her belly, you could die if you eat it?"

"Bubba, you ain't lyin'," said Jimbo, cleaning the blood off his machete in the water.

"This lake would be perfect if twern't for gars and snappin' turtles. A real par'dise."

"True, but least for now we got ourselves an ice chest of fish an' a big ol' lunker to bring home and fry."

"Well now, that's a good way to put it. I learnt from you twice today, Jimbo," said Gumbo. "Now, let's get these home to Momma. She gon' be pleased."

Questions

1. There are several violent images in the story. What are they? Why is this necessary, given the meaning of the parable?

2. What qualities do Jimbo and Gumbo praise in the fish?

3. What do the fish they keep all have in common? What about the ones they don't?

4. Likewise, on what basis do humans "pass through" judgment?

5. Did you read this after reading "Beautiful Boy," the story based on the parable of the Wicked Tenants? How might the meaning of this story make it an appropriate follow up?

Subversive Stories

THE PARABLE OF THE WEEDS
Matthew 13:24-30

"The kingdom of heaven may be compared to a man who sowed good seed in his field, but while his men were sleeping, his enemy came and sowed weeds among the wheat and went away. So when the plants came up and bore grain, then the weeds appeared also. And the servants of the master of the house came and said to him, 'Master, did you not sow good seed in your field? How then does it have weeds?' He said to them, 'An enemy has done this.' So the servants said to him, 'Then do you want us to go and gather them?' But he said, 'No, lest in gathering the weeds you root up the wheat along with them. Let both grow together until the harvest, and at harvest time I will tell the reapers, "Gather the weeds first and bind them in bundles to be burned, but gather the wheat into my barn."'"

Where Two or More Are Gathered

"Brother John, I need to warn you before the service this morning."

"Warn? Why, what's wrong?" I said.

"We have a saying in this country." Aung held up two crooked fingers. "'Where two or more are gathered in the name of Christ, the government is in their midst.'"

"I see." I thought for a moment. "As in, spies?"

"Yes, brother."

"How do you know?" My palms began to sweat.

"I know." He blinked and nodded once. "Let me ask you. In your visit here this week, how many times have you spoken to a group?"

"Four, no . . . five times."

"Then the government has already heard you speak five times."

"Aung, those were your friends, that was your orphanage I spoke to. Orphans."

"I know."

"You don't trust them?"

"I love them all, but no, I only trust some."

"Even your orphans? They're just kids."

"Yes," he said, resolute.

"I'm sure there's some truth in what you're saying but, I don't know, it seems a little, I hate to say it . . . paranoid."

"Ah, I'm not offended, brother. I know it's different in America. I will give you a few examples. Five years ago, one of our orphans, Ko, was at school, and he was taken out of class and brought to the principal's office. Now, the schools here are mainly run by the government. And the principal said to him, 'Little Ko, we want to make you a deal. Every Monday, you will meet with me and tell me what Mr. Aung says in your worship service on Sunday.'

"Poor Ko said, 'Why would I do that? Pastor Aung cares for me.'

"The principal said to him, 'Because if you don't you will be guilty of insubordination. Little Ko, do you know the punishment for insubordination?' Ko shook his head. 'Give me your hand,' the principal said to him. 'Both of them.' Ko put his hands forward. The principal took a marker and drew a line across his wrists. 'Do you see these lines, Little Ko?' Ko nodded. 'That is where your hands will be cut off for insubordination.'

"Now, brother John, what do you think poor Ko did for the next five years?"

I closed my eyes and nodded. "He spied."

"Yes, my friend. He spied. Now, I will tell you another story. For about twenty years, a man named Thein and his family have come to the church service in our home. I don't think he has ever missed a Sunday. When there is a need, he serves. He is hospitable and shares his food and possessions. He knows his Bible well. He has even given money to the Bible college. If you met him, you would think to yourself, 'Behold, a Burmese in whom there is no guile.' But guess what, brother?"

"What?"

"One day Thein's sister came to us. She also worships in my home. And she says to me, 'Ah, pastor Aung, my brother is a spy. He has been a government informant for many years, for all this time. I just found out. They pay him double what he makes at the market to collect information about you.'"

"Good grief, Aung, that's terrible."

"Yes, and there are other stories I could tell you."

"I'm sorry for doubting you. Forgive me."

"Of course," he nodded.

"So, what do you do about them?" I said.

"About who?"

"The spies. The informants."

"Do? There is nothing to do."

"You can't tell me you just let them stay among you."

"Oh yes, that is the only option. You have already preached to Ko in the orphanage earlier this week, and you will meet Thein and his family in just a little while at morning worship. And I promise you, they are not the only spies."

"How could you just let them stay?"

"What would you like me to do?"

"Confront them! Excommunicate them from the church. Aung, these are your enemies. They want to destroy you. They want to see the kingdom burn."

"What do you think would happen if I confronted Ko? Eh, brother?"

"I don't know."

"At the very least, Ko would lose his hands. And probably disappear altogether. And then they would recruit and corrupt another of my orphans."

I nodded slowly.

"And Thein, if I kicked him and his family out of the church, what do you think might happen to our beloved little congregation?"

I shook my head.

"At best, another spy would join us. But more likely, the regime would see it as a threat, as defiance. Our home would be invaded the next Sunday, our leaders imprisoned and members beaten for illegal religious activity, and our home repossessed by the government. Or, if they did not want it, they would set fire to it."

"I understand."

"At least this way, keeping them in our midst, the work of God can continue. Alongside Ko are other orphans who are growing up into men of God, into women who love the Lord Jesus. By allowing Thein to worship with us, we can continue giving the Lord the honor he is due, and his church is able to multiply and bear fruit in this dark part of the earth. Think of it, brother. So what if they are spying? What information will they pass along to their superiors, eh? That we care for orphans? That we pray for daily bread? That we believe in the resurrection from the dead? I have nothing to hide, brother. I think it is best to assume that the enemy is always among us, to account for that as we work, and not waste time trying to sort out the wheat from the weeds. A Day is coming when the Lord himself will sort it all out. I will leave it to him. In the meantime, I will care for orphans and preach the gospel."

"I understand."

"You may not have government spies in your churches, my friend, but make no mistake, even in America, where two or more are gathered, the Enemy is in your midst. The Enemy takes many forms. And neither you nor I are wise enough to say for sure who is who. And don't forget, even your own heart will deceive you as an angel of light. Who but the Lord is trustworthy?"

I was silent, soaking it all in.

"Well," he looked at his watch. "It is time for the service. Don't worry about Thein. Just preach the gospel, brother, even to your enemies." He laughed and poked me in the chest with his short, crooked finger. "And especially to the enemy within."

Questions

1. In the country the story takes place (Myanmar), the government has placed or corrupted people in Aung's congregation ("weeds"). What reality does this reflect about the church at large?

2. Aung is not overly worried about the spies in their midst (similar to the master). How does this speak to our distress over people and problems within the church?

3. The master points his distressed servants to the coming harvest. How does this help us when we are disturbed or angry over sin and evil?

4. People's true natures will be revealed at the return of Christ, at judgment. Why is this not possible now?

5. In what way is your heart a field of wheat and weeds?

Subversive Stories

The Parable of the Ten Virgins
Matthew 25:1-13

"Then the kingdom of heaven will be like ten virgins who took their lamps and went to meet the bridegroom. Five of them were foolish, and five were wise. For when the foolish took their lamps, they took no oil with them, but the wise took flasks of oil with their lamps. As the bridegroom was delayed, they all became drowsy and slept. But at midnight there was a cry, 'Here is the bridegroom! Come out to meet him.' Then all those virgins rose and trimmed their lamps. And the foolish said to the wise, 'Give us some of your oil, for our lamps are going out.' But the wise answered, saying, 'Since there will not be enough for us and for you, go rather to the dealers and buy for yourselves.' And while they were going to buy, the bridegroom came, and those who were ready went in with him to the marriage feast, and the door was shut. Afterward the other virgins came also, saying, 'Lord, lord, open to us.' But he answered, 'Truly, I say to you, I do not know you.' Watch therefore, for you know neither the day nor the hour."

The Day of the Dove Hunt

For many years of my childhood, I had been led to believe that Labor Day weekend was a national holiday set aside for hunting dove, just as Easter was set aside for hunting eggs. My family awaited the Day as we did any other holiday, planning and discussing it with eager anticipation.

The night before, Dad retrieved our shotguns from the gun safe in his closet. He cleared off the kitchen table and laid an old bed sheet on it. Dad had an old Remington with a wood stock that he'd had since he was a boy. My brother Paul had recently gotten a black Browning 12 gauge with a golden trigger for his sixteenth birthday. Only ten years old, this was the first year I would be allowed to hunt in the field. I would be using Dad's single shot .410, which kicked like a mule and weighed as much as one too. It had been my grandfather's when he was a boy and still worked perfectly, having been preserved over the decades. Since last year's hunt I had been practicing with clay pigeons. According to Dad, I was ready. Paul thought I needed to wait another year.

Dad laid out the guns on the covered kitchen table, disassembling various parts. I helped him oil and clean the guns while my brother brought other items from the bedroom closet. When the guns were clean and the barrels almost blue with oil, we put them in their cases. We each carried our own to the truck in the garage. Laying the case in the truck bed next to theirs, I felt like I finally belonged, a true hunter. I said something to that effect and was quickly rebuffed by my brother, who told me I wasn't a hunter until I actually killed something.

While Dad cleaned out the truck, Paul and I brought out an armful of shotgun shell boxes, but Dad made us take them back to the closet. "Those are for duck, not dove," he said. We brought the right ones and laid them in the army surplus bag. I also added three boxes of .410 shells. We loaded the truck bed with various items: bags, seats, buckets, a couple of decoys, shooting earmuffs, and an Igloo filled with ice and drinks. Back inside we laid our camouflage on the floor alongside our hats and boots. I went ahead and slid a box of candy into the pocket of my pants so I didn't forget. Finally, I turned off the lights and laid down, staring at the ceiling for what seemed like ages.

I'm not sure that I ever actually fell asleep, anxious with waiting. Yet, I must have, because I awoke to Dad's hand on my back. "Time to go, hunter," he said. Half-dead, I put on my clothes, ate a cold biscuit with some orange juice, and got in the car. Paul got in and finally, Dad. Before we left Dad went through a mental checklist. Finally, the truck pulled quietly out of the driveway and eventually found its way in the dark to a winding country road. The clock on the truck console said 4:35 am. I could smell my dad's coffee, which had made a little circle of fog on the windshield. I could also smell my brother's rancid breath, which he kept blowing onto the window like a dragon, so he could draw in the condensation. I laid on my side in the back seat and dozed.

A while later I woke when the truck pulled to a stop. I yawned, opened the door and was greeted by the first cool morning since spring. Far outside of the city now, the sky was blacker, the stars brighter. It was utterly still and silent outside. The crickets and owls had ceased their sounds, and the birds and squirrels had not yet stirred. We walked into our great uncle's house, a farmer who hosted the hunt each year.

Uncle Phil greeted us at the door, shaking our hands. "Come on in, fellas." We gathered in the kitchen. Besides us, there were two others, my dad's cousin, Richie, and his daughter, Gina. Gina had a reddish golden retriever next to her, who came up to us and greeted us, wagging his tail. "Coffee's hot if you want it," Uncle Phil said.

"Where's everyone else?" Paul asked.

"Oh, you know how it is. They'll be here."

We stood around the kitchen island, the men talking about their wives, about the upcoming football season, about last year's hunt. Finally, a couple of Uncle Phil's neighbors came in the door. "Come on in, y'all. Coffee's hot. It's almost time." They came into the kitchen wearing bright red and neon yellow rather than camouflage. "Woo! Gonna blind someone with all that color," he said.

One of them responded, "The internet said rather than hiding with camo you can attract 'em with color. Like a bull."

We all laughed except for the neighbors. Uncle Phil said,

"What's the internet know about huntin' birds?" He laughed again and excused himself to the bathroom.

After a few more minutes of small talk, Uncle Phil came back, looked at his watch, and then out the window. "Well, sky's starting to lighten a bit. I guess we'd better get goin'. Now listen, as far as the hunt today —"

The door opened, and he turned. "Hey! Come on in. You just 'bout missed the boat." Uncle Phil's farmhand came inside with his son, who was staring down at his phone, playing a game. "Alright, where was I? The hunt today. Listen, the weather —"

The door opened again, Uncle Phil turned, frustrated. "Dadgum," he said. "I thought I said five thirty?" A man came into the kitchen, looking hungover. "I'll make it quick. The weather's been funny lately. The cool front came in with some rain last night. That's a coin toss, fellas. Could make for a great hunt but could be a dud. Hard to tell."

The neighbors groaned. The farmhand muttered something to his son. The man who came in last with the long face and bloodshot eyes cursed, spat in the kitchen sink, and said, "I wouldn've even come if I'da knowed it rained."

Uncle Phil shrugged and smiled. "We'll see. All I know is I got a field of sunflowers that I planted and left unharvested just for you. So, get on out there and let's have a good, safe hunt. And don't shoot no low birds 'less you want to shoot each other." He took off his hat and prayed for the hunt. Then we left for the field.

We got to the field of sunflowers and parked under a large sycamore near the entrance. Dad and Paul looked around and decided on a spot to hunt from. We laid some of our gear onto our backs and shoulders, and took the rest in our hands, heading out alongside Richie, Gina, and the neighbors. We passed the farmhand's truck and saw that he and his son were both on their phones. We passed the man with the bloodshot eyes, whose truck was still on and windows rolled down. He had his feet up on the dashboard, his hat over his eyes. "Y'all call me when they come," he said, rolling up his windows.

We stepped through the moist field until we got to a spot Dad picked out, maybe three hundred yards away from the truck. "You see," he said to me, "Doves like to follow lines - fences, crop rows, power lines. Any kind of line." Richie and Gina and their dog walked past us and set up a little further down, on the edge of the field. We loaded our guns and sat down on our foldout stools. When my brother wasn't looking, I put a handful of candy from my pocket into my mouth. The neighbors were across the field from us, facing us. Even in the dim light they stood out in their bright colored clothing among the brown sunflower stalks.

The sky was now lavender gray, the sun not yet above the horizon of trees. The gun felt cold in my hands. "There's going to be birds, right Dad?" I said.

"I think so."

I couldn't bear the wait. After a few minutes I said, "How do you know?"

"Would you chill?" Paul said. "They'll be here. Just be ready." I kicked his boot and made a face at him.

"Is that a dove?" I asked, pointing.

"No," Paul said.

A few minutes later. "That?" I said.

"That's a buzzard, son," Dad said.

I laid down my gun and took out my pocketknife. I was trying to throw it at the ground and make the blade stick. After a while I stood up. "Can I go talk to Gina?"

"Sure," Dad said, looking up at the sky. I began to walk off. "Son," he said. I looked at him. "Take your gun."

I put the .410 with its sling on my shoulder and walked down to Gina. "Hey," I said. "You think it's going to be a dud? Like that guy said?" She was wearing camo overalls with a tan shirt. Her auburn hair was braided and ran down her back, ending in a camouflage bow.

"Daddy says it's gonna be a good one. He says a little cool rain is good luck. 'Stirs 'em up and gets 'em moving.' Ain't that right, Daddy?" He nodded, not taking his eyes from the sky. She stroked the dog's head. "Humphrey here thinks it'll be a good one. Look at 'em. He's ready, a real huntin' dog." She looked over my shoulder. "Hey, I think your daddy's calling you." I turned and saw Dad waving me back in the dim light.

I ran back to him. "Get down, son. Look." He pointed to the east. The sun was just coming above the horizon, setting clouds aflame. It cast a reddish light, about the color of Gina's dog, onto the field. Dad's face was glowing with it.

"Yeah, pretty sunrise," I said.

"No, dummy," Paul said. "Birds."

I looked closer. The distance and the light made it almost impossible to see, but finally I found them. Just above the rising sun, they looked like fleas moving across the sky.

I felt a little clammy and queasy. In years past, I was only allowed to sit and watch and to help retrieve fallen birds. This year, though, I was not an observer; I had the same chance to hunt as the rest of them. But that meant I also had the potential to mess it up. What if I couldn't hit any? What if I shot a chickadee by mistake? What if I —

"Bird!" Gina called from behind us.

Dad lifted his shotgun to his shoulder and fired. *Boom! Tick.* A bird fell. *Boom! Tick. Boom!* Another fell into the field. I rose to retrieve them, but Dad held his arm out, stopping me. "Wait. Get your gun up."

While Dad was reloading, several doves came over us, bluish gray, their wings curved gracefully and tails red with the sunrise.

Paul stood and shot three times, one falling out of the sky. Gina and Richie were shooting behind me. Humphrey was sprinting back and forth to them with birds in his mouth. I looked up. A swarm of doves were flying straight at us. Dad looked back at me, loading his gun. "Go ahead, son. You've prepared for this. You're ready."

I lifted my gun into the air. I chose a dove and tried to follow it, but it was too quick. I didn't know how I'd hold the gun up like that for much longer, heavy as it was. I finally just pointed at a cluster of birds and fired. One of them went limp, a puff of feathers in the air behind it. It crashed to the ground with a little thump.

"Hey! You did it!" Paul said. He smiled and patted me on the back. "You're a real hunter now, little brother." I looked at him and laughed, a little surprised. He raised his gun and shot twice more in the sky.

I popped the empty cartridge out of my .410 and loaded a new one. After three more shots, I got another bird. After that, I shot one that had been wounded and was fluttering around near the fence.

I looked up and saw the neighbors running to us from across the field. Dad and Paul kept shooting, birds raining down around us into the sunflower stalks and the mud.

The neighbors came up to Dad, breathing heavily. "Y'all got some shells we can borrow? Genius here brought 20 gauge shells instead of 12."

"Sorry fellas," Dad said without looking at him. *Boom! Tick.* Another bird fell. "Paul and I have gone through two boxes already. Two boxes *each*. But I have a 20 gauge in the back of my truck you can use with your shells. Feel free. Oh, and tell the loafers they're missing the action."

Just as Dad said it, I saw the farmhand and his son hurrying out into the field. They threw their things down and the man started to load his gun. A dove came over him and he raised his firearm, but nothing happened. He took his gun off his shoulder and looked at it. He checked in the chamber, and then lifted it to his shoulder and tried again. Nothing. He cursed and ran across the field to Gina and Richie.

When the birds slowed for a moment, Richie's voice carried across the field, "Good grief, fella! When's the last time you oiled and cleaned this thing?"

For the next five minutes the birds continue to flock to the field. Dad and Paul knocked one after another out of the sky. I got two more for a total of five. Dad laughed and set his gun down. "I think we hit the legal limit several birds ago, Paul. We better stop before the game warden comes. We need to retrieve them all anyway."

The neighbors had finally gotten back with the right gun for their shells, and Dad let the farmhand borrow his gun. But, unfortunately for them, as soon as we began searching the fields, the birds tapered off, and before long stopped altogether.

"I'm sure more will come," the farmhand said to his son, who was playing on his phone once again.

We found thirty-three fallen birds ourselves, stuffing them in our bags, and recruited Humphrey to track down the last handful. In all, eighteen for Dad, fifteen for Paul, and five for me.

"Well done, son," Dad said, thumping me in the chest. "I knew you were a hunter, but I didn't know you were such a *fine* hunter."

I grinned, feeling that my whole existence in the world had just been justified. A *fine* hunter, he had said.

We picked up our gear, which felt lighter now despite being heavy with game. "Let's go clean our birds," Dad said.

On the way back we passed the truck of the man with the bloodshot eyes. Dad knocked on the window, startling him from sleep. He lifted his cap, took his feet off the dashboard, and rolled down the window. A sour smell wafted out.

"Might want to get out there," Dad said. "We hit our limits and the sun's barely up."

The man cursed and spat and turned his truck off. "I guess the cool and the rain turned to our favor," Dad said to him as he rummaged through his truck cabin for his hunting gear. We started to gut and clean the birds with Richie and Gina, while the man joined the other four in the field. They all stood looking at the sky, waiting for the birds to come again. There was not a dove in sight.

"They ain't too good o' hunters, Daddy," Gina said.

"They ain't hunters at all, honey. They just playin' at it. A hunter would'a been ready, rain or shine."

Questions

1. Which hunters are wise in the story? Which are foolish? Give examples of each.

2. What's the main difference between the two types of hunters? How does this relate to the return of Christ, which is at the heart of this parable?

3. Describe the moments the boy narrating the story is affirmed as a "hunter." What does this have to do with judgment?

4. Name the ways that the "wise" hunters in the story prepared for the hunt. Likewise, how should you prepare and be ready for the return of Christ?

5. The return of Christ is often spoken of with fear and dread ("Apocalypse" and "Armageddon"), yet the Bible speaks of it as the believer's greatest hope and a day of joy. How do you feel about his return? Why?

ABOUT THE AUTHOR

David Elston lives in Shreveport, Louisiana, his hometown, with his wife Jessica and three children - Judah, Frances, and Hope. When David is not moonlighting as a writer, he works as Executive Director and Counselor at Shreveport Biblical Counseling. He is ordained as a ruling elder at Grace Presbyterian (PCA). David has also written *Resurrecting Beauty: A Portrait of Jesus Christ* and a novel called *The Inlet*.

David enjoys hearing from readers. Feel free to email him with questions and comments at davidbelston@gmail.com.

ABOUT SBC

Shreveport Biblical Counseling aims to serve and equip the church in Shreveport through the ministry of biblical counseling. We accomplish this mission in three ways:

1. Counseling individuals, marriages and families.
2. Training and consulting with church leaders to help care for their members.
3. Writing that applies and illustrates the wisdom and grace of God.

All profits from the sale of this book go directly to Shreveport Biblical Counseling, a 501(c)(3) non-profit. If you'd like to see us produce more books like this, consider donating to our writing ministry.

www.shrevebc.com

670 Albemarle Dr. Shreveport, LA 71106

(318) 200-0750 | admin@shrevebc.com